KAREN D. NEAL

AND

PENSIVE PUBLISHING

PRESENTS:

RENEE BLACK'S

HIDDEN DESIRES: REVEALED

Printed in the United States of America

First Printing, 2015

Cover Design by: Asoral

Edited by: Karen N. Cummings

Table of Contents

And So It Begins   5

Chapter 1   8

Chapter 2   26

Chapter 3   41

Chapter 4   55

Chapter 5   78

Chapter 6   95

Chapter 7   107

Chapter 8   120

Chapter 9   135

Chapter 10   143

Chapter 11   159

Chapter 12   181

Chapter 13   197

Acknowledgments

I would like to take this opportunity to thank my family and friends for supporting me through this process. To Linda, my best friend, thank you for being patient with me, and giving me plenty of alone/quiet time, and support when I needed it. TC, I'd like to thank you for inspiring me to write through my pain and then helping me with some editing. Stephanie, my daughter, I can't say enough! Thanks for being you and going with me on this roller coaster called life, although you really didn't have a choice. You truly are one in a trillion. Thank you, Karen D. Neal, for believing in me and helping me through this journey of having my voice heard. LJ Thomas, thank you so much for designing a wonderful book cover.

I dedicate this book to the memory of Amber Sunshine Crosby. I never thought I could live without you, but I am doing just fine; exactly as you said I would. Thank you for coming to me in dreams when I need a pick-me-up. You will always be the Sunshine of my life.

June 26, 1975 – August 4, 2009

Phenix Roze

And So It Begins

Nightlife at the Golden Ridge Inn was basically the only entertainment offered in the small town and of course the 24-hour Super Wal-Mart served as the town mall. The crowd was a mixture of ages, ranging from twenty-one to seventy-three. The smell of smoke and liquor permeated the air as laughter and chatter could be heard over the huge variety of music, which varied from Motown, Classic Rock, and Today's Hits. There were several round tables encircling the dance floor with a myriad of cliques forming around most of them. A group of young ladies were seated at the bar in their own world of entertainment on this night.

Allison, Sarah, Erica, Monya, and Beulah were sitting together. Beulah was the only one who seemed out of place with the rest. She was drinking a virgin drink instead of the alcoholic laced pretty cocktail, or the hard stuff that seemed free-flowing tonight. She was constantly looking around as if paranoid. She knew that the girls had only invited her out tonight to be nice. The other girls were relaxed and saying hello to other patrons as they'd pass by. Monya and Erica were best friends. They were the spontaneous characters of the crew. Sarah was the strong silent type, with the determination to be her best self; even if it meant she had to forgo her own desires. Allison was the least experienced, all around. She had only had a few serious relationships and was naive to the world around her, almost as if she'd been hidden in an invisibility cloak while growing up. Allison, Erica, and Monya danced, as Sarah looked on with a slightly nervous smile.

They all took turns dancing with Merv, an older gentleman that had long been known to be the town drunk, and very unlucky with the ladies. He was wearing a silk, long-sleeved, flowery shirt that was red and white, khaki corduroy pants, and a brown pair of worn out biker boots. The ladies' had to be mindful of his steps while dancing with him. He was unsteady and tripping over their feet. He was grinning and singing in their ears. When Allison danced with him he slid his hand over her butt, and she slapped his face. A few of the other people in the bar laughed out loud.

Sarah noticed a few guys staring at Allison as she was dancing. It made her feel uncomfortable. She passed it off as her caution to what the male species was capable of. Females were malicious sometimes but not as violent as men could be. Perhaps that is one of the reasons she chose the company of women rather than men. She knew it was only a matter of time before some horrible crime was committed against a female, or females, in this town. That thought made her appreciate the fact that not everyone knew of her sexuality. Deep in thought, she didn't realize the girls had returned to the bar and the conversation that ensued brought her out of her thoughts.

"My husband is very loving and gentle in bed." Monya said, with a drunken glaze in her eye.

Erica slammed her hand down on the bar. "Well, Chad is all over the place! It's like he is so excited he can't slow down long enough to make sure I'm getting mine too."

"Well, I prefer a little domineerin' myself. I want someone to come in while I'm sleepin' and have their way with me, but not in a violent way. Oh my God! I've never said that out loud! I had way too many Grateful Dead's tonight!" Ali quickly covered her mouth.

They all erupted into laughter, including the bartender, the guy at the end of the bar, and the guys at the table to the right of them. Allison's eyes became huge and she swiftly looked down at the floor. The other gals gasped and exploded with laughter. Ali's face flushed. Sarah stopped snickering and wrapped her arm around Allison's shoulder.

"I need a cigarette. Sarah, will you come with me outside please?" Sarah and Ali quickly left the building.

1

"He was gentle with you?" A look of disbelief spread across the officer's face. He'd never come across a rape that was not meant to over-power and threaten, at least in some way.

"Yeah, I mean it was completely different from what you see on TV or the news," she replied. She didn't know what to think.

The two of them stared at each other in confusion.

Deputy Sparks closely watched Allison. She wasn't showing any of the classic signs of rape. She had even accepted his hand, without a flinch, when he helped her up on the stretcher. She didn't seem traumatized at all. In fact, her demeanor was quite calm. He was beginning to think she was an attention seeker.

Her mind's eye flashed on the rapist's eyes. They were hazel green, very still, almost caring.

The deputy saw her eyebrows furl. "Did you just remember something?"

"Yes. His eyes were hazel green," she offered.

Sparks adjusted his belt. Beads of sweat were resting on his temples. It had been at least four years since he'd worked a rape case. It still bothered him that women could be made to feel so vulnerable by a jerk, plus, the beeping of the machines was stressing him out. He noticed Ms. Carter picking at her fingernails. He felt more empathy for the confused young lady, and regained his patience. Tenderly, he asked, "Ma'am, I know this is difficult. Is there anyone ya want me to call for ya?"

She gently shook her head as she said, "No, I'm okay." She looked back down at her feet. Her toenails could use a re-paint. Ali wondered what it would be like to have Sarah there to support her. Would it be calming or embarrassing? She decided to chance it. "Well, actually I'd be more comfortable if I could call Sarah. She'll support me."

"Alright." Sparks thought every rape victim needed someone to talk to, and the way she was picking at her hands made him realize she was definitely uncomfortable.

Ali curled her toes under and hoped no one had paid attention to them. She pulled out her cell phone and made the call. It was short and sweet. She only told Sarah that she was at the Emergency Room and needed her.

"Well ma'am, I'm sorry to push ya, but I really need to know exactly what happened." David Sparks was an honorable and virtuous man. He believed that the justice system could work for anyone that was willing to trust it. It was engrained in him from birth, as his father and grandfather both retired from the department. In this circumstance however, he was fumbling for the right words to say, to this already frightened girl. She seemed to be very nervous, and withdrawn, as he'd seen in so many other victims before. He witnessed her looking down and tucking her feet under the stretcher, as her hands lay folded in her lap. He needed to find this guy and bring some peace to this child's mind. After seventeen years on the force he had wonderful interrogation skills, but what he needed now were interviewing skills. He thought back to his multiple trainings. The first rule is to keep a soft, level tone, to capture stability. Secondly, keep a physical distance of three feet, so as not to cause any undue stress.

"I know you need the details," she said. Ali looked at the officer intently, and then continued, "You don't believe me. I can tell by the look on your face." She couldn't believe he was an officer of the justice system but seemed to be passing judgment without having all the evidence. Then again, he was a male, and men in her neck of the woods tended to stick together.

"No ma'am, that's not it." Was he being insensitive? He knew each individual case and victim was different and needed different approaches, but which way should he go from here?

"Yes it is damn it!" Allison was flustered and lashing out. Ali was ready for a cigarette. She couldn't believe she yelled at an officer of the law. That was completely out of character for her. It reminded her of the time she was six years old and her uncle hugged her at a family get-together. She pushed him away and made a hissing noise at him. He smiled then looked around to see who was watching them. Apparently no one was. He called her a "little bitch", and then walked away. A year earlier she had confessed to her mother that he had been touching her inappropriately and making her touch him, but she wasn't believed. Her mother had furled her eyebrows and guffawed, and then said, "My, what an imagination we have?" Allison was heart-broken. From that day forward she didn't trust her mother.

That was the first time she'd rebelled against authority. This was the second. The first time came out of anger and self-preservation. As the years passed she didn't speak to that uncle. Her mom would sometimes tell her that she reminded her of him, but Betty didn't realize how deeply that offended Ali. She tried to forget about it for years, and finally was able to suppress her anger. She didn't speak to him unless he spoke to her. He seemed to have forgotten all about acting on his desires for his niece when he was sixteen, but those actions effected aspects of her entire life. Ali's thoughts put a sad look on her face, as she stared at Deputy Sparks' belt buckle. She didn't actually see it though; her mind was wandering.

Sparks took a deep breath to regroup, and stay composed. He kindly suggested that she start from the top and include all the aspects she could remember. "The rapist's identity might be in the smallest detail," he encouraged.

She nodded. His tone eased her a bit. "Okay, well, like any Tuesday, I went to Ladies' Night, at the Golden Ridge Inn. I meet a few of my co-workers there. It was just a normal night of dancin', talkin', drinkin', flirtin' with the guys, and just hangin' out."

Officer Sparks interrupted her. "Did ya notice any of the men payin' special attention to ya, starin' at ya, anyone make ya feel uncomfortable, or did ya have harsh words with anyone?" He needed a suspect to investigate.

Allison's eyebrows crimpled together as she was in deep thought. She peered at the ceiling, and then began searching the small room with her eyes, as if that would give her answers. She noticed one of the cabinet doors was slightly ajar. Hospitals sure did come off as boring and sterile. The whole room was off-white, except for the silver sink, with its high arching faucet. She fought the urge to get up and close the cabinet; she didn't want to come off as odd. Looking back at Sparks, she finally responded, "I don't remember anything out of the ordinary, but I told ya I was drinkin'. I got a little tipsy. I did slap Merv 'cause he touched my butt, but I'm pretty sure it wasn't him. He could barely stand. I didn't drive myself home either. My friend, Sarah, drove me."

"Mm-hmm, and what time…" he was interrupted by a nurse.

"Officer I have the results you've been waitin' on." The nurse gave Allison a quick sympathetic smile.

Ali smiled back. There was kindness in the nurse's brown eyes. The dinosaurs on her scrubs were playing baseball, which made Allison smirk. The nurse's hair was brown with a top layer of blonde, and her voice was confident, yet compassionate. She appeared to be in her early forties, and Ali admired how her hair naturally flowed away from her face, and behind her ears; it made Ali think of Samantha's hair, from Bewitched. She was attractive, and looked to be a gentle soul.

"Yes ma'am," he answered, then excused himself from the room. He slowly limped out, favoring his right side. Suddenly he swung back around, in the door frame. "Oh! Ms. Carter, do ya have any bruises, cuts, scratches, or marks that we need to take a picture of?"

Allison gritted her teeth, batted her eyelashes, and spoke through a fake smile, "I told ya he didn't hurt me in ANY way!" Then she dropped her cheeks, letting the smile disappear, rolled her eyes, and let out a sigh of frustration. Just when she thought she was making headway with this guy, he slipped back into the asshole role.

Sensing the obvious tension, Nurse Roberts quickly interjected, "Hon, why don't ya go on ahead and get dressed. We got everything we need."

As soon as the door closed, Allison slid off the bed and got dressed hurriedly. She didn't want anyone coming in on her, and as far as she was concerned, the curtain wasn't doing a good enough job. The cabinet door was still drawing her attention so she closed it, and felt a little relief. She was anxious to find out the results of the tests. Ali had been waiting for over an hour. That's an hour of looking at the same four boring walls; same boring ceiling, taking intrusive tests, and she still wanted a cigarette. She could almost taste the menthol on her tongue. She was anxious to say the least. She couldn't wait for Sarah to get there, mostly, but she had reservations about it too. She was looking forward to the peace she got from being in Sarah's presence, but also felt an embarrassment because Sarah would hear very intimate details about her, sexually.

Sparks was waiting just outside of the nurse's station for the doctor to fill him in, but Nurse Roberts showed up instead.

"The doctor had an emergency stab victim that was brought in", she said as she opened the metal chart she was holding. "Basically, there is no sign of semen, tearin', bruises, cuts, scrapes, nothin' to suggest rape, except the tiny chafe marks on her wrists."

His eyebrows furled. "So…she wasn't raped?" Why would someone come to the ER with a crazy story like that?

"Well, there are signs of sexual contact, although I can't say with one hundred percent certainty that it was rape. There was, however, a small amount of bacteria on her uterine wall."

Sparks was confused. He crinkled his nose up.

Nurse Roberts detected his confusion, due to the look on his face. "Well both men and women have a "tell" that exposes sexual contact or release. You see, a male's penis will stiffen, at least partially, when exposed to air, on any given day; UNLESS, he's had sexual release within the last 4 to 6 hours. Then, there might be some movement, like a twitch here and there, but it won't stiffen completely. Now, if a male has anal intercourse, it's the same as if a female does. There will be redness, swellin', busted capillaries, and possibly even small flakes of dried blood from the tearin'."

A look of disgust cropped up on Sparks' face. "Please, move on to the female's vaginal area", he said, with a compelling tone.

She promptly obliged. "Sorry," she said, through a giggle. "When a female has sexual contact/release, there is an artery that becomes engorged. The clitoris is attached to it, which is why it can elicit multiple orgasms. It can remain engorged for up to twelve hours. That is how I know that she definitely had sexual contact."

Sparks responded with, "Okay, so she had sex, but was it rape? There are no physical signs of rape, and she sure ain't showin' any emotional signs. I…I just don't get it."

Nurse Denise Roberts had more experience with rape victims than he did. She was a charge nurse, which means all the other nurses answer to her, and she provides them with any information they may need. She enjoyed using her experience and medical knowledge to help others. She felt duty bound to express her opinion, and knew that if she didn't she'd regret it.

She had to make him understand her point of view. "Seriously…I've dealt with a lot of rape victims, and they're all different. She definitely had sexual contact. There was an alien strand of bacteria in her vagina. She didn't name an attacker…AND she's cooperatin' completely. Yeah, it is a rare case, but I do believe she was raped. Why else would she put herself through all of this? What? For attention? I don't think so. If it was attention she wanted she'd be layin' it on real thick, and she's not even cryin'."

Sparks nodded his head. Her point came through loud and clear. At that moment his phone rang. He excused himself from the conversation, pulled his cell phone out of its holster, and took three steps away. Sparks mainly listened, but also asked a few questions. As the call ended he walked back toward Nurse Roberts.

"Well apparently, the technicians of our Crime Scene Unit have scoured every inch of her house. They found no actual semen, or DNA. There was only a miniscule amount of fluid that was separated from what we assume to be Ms. Carter's fluids. I guess he wore a condom, I mean this guy is good. There was no evidence of a break-in or robbery. However, the scarves that were used to tie her hands were still hangin' from the headboard. They're bein' taken to the lab for tests. If there is any trace evidence they'll find it."

"Okay," replied Nurse Roberts. "Well, she's ready to go unless ya need her for somethin' else."

"Yeah, I need just a few more minutes with her. I'm bein' thorough. This is a rare case and I can't miss a beat on this one." He felt he needed to justify himself after thinking she was an attention seeker.

The nurse smiled and said, "It's good to see that the law can be human. Take care of her and if ya need anything else just holler."

With a softened look of compassion, Sparks said, "Will do." Then he stepped back to the door of Allison's room.

"Are you dressed Ms. Carter?"

"Yes," Ali's voice came from the other side of the door; her patience was wearing thin.

He stepped in. "Okay Ms. Carter. Here's the deal. I really need the whole story, and look, I'm sorry if it seemed like I didn't believe ya before. It's just that I've never come across a case like this, and it has me baffled."

Validation made Allison feel more at ease. "Finally," she paused, and breathed a sigh of relief. "Look I want to know about the STD tests first. If I have somethin' I need to know." She was afraid that he had given her something terrible, other than the possibility of being pregnant.

"Oh. Hang on just a minute." He stepped back out into the hall and motioned for the nurse to come back. "Can you tell her what the tests showed so she can stop worrying?"

"Well…you have nothing to worry about sweetie. They all came back negative, but it's always best to be tested a few months out also, just to make double sure." Nurse Roberts smiled and walked out of the door.

A look of relief spread across Allison's face as she dropped her shoulders and took a deep breath. "Thank God! I don't know how this happened to me, or why, but I was startin' to feel like I was totally in this alone. Thank you for sayin' you believe me." Her lips turned up just at the corners.

"Ms. Carter, the hospital can provide ya with a rape counselor. I can request one if you'd like." Sparks wanted to make sure he included all information.

Allison shook her head. "Look, the nurse already offered me one, a long time ago. I said no." She looked down at the floor again, and then continued, "My mom is a counselor at Placid Behavioral Health. I know all about self-help groups, treatments, and all that stuff. I just don't relish the thought of talkin' about this with a stranger okay? Besides, they'll just talk about me after I leave." She heard her mom complaining about how staff would talk about patients after they'd left, and how unethical it was.

"Oh, okay. Well, just know that is an option, however they do need this room, but I still have questions for ya. Would ya like to go to the station or just move to another room here? There is an empty office we can use."

"Well I'm already here." What was the point of going down to the station at this time of morning?

Sparks nodded his head in agreement. "Okay, hold on I'll go get it ready."

As he exited the room again, her cell phone buzzed. Sarah sent a text that read, "*B there in 10 mins. Hope u r ok.*" Ali couldn't wait to see Sarah. She knew she could count on her. Sarah had been there for her when her father died, when Justin left her, and when she had a tumor removed from her uterus. She was also there for Sarah when Marie broke up with her, the last time. Her feelings for Sarah had changed over the last six months or so. She was perplexed, excited, and curious about her, and for some reason she felt it even more so tonight. It was like the rape had given her some sort of sexual confidence, but she was still scared. Adventurous fantasies were running through her mind. She'd never had any kind of physical contact with a female, but frequently wondered about it, especially with Sarah. Of course, Ali thought it was only because she knew Sarah was a lesbian, and because they were close. She didn't consider herself gay, just curious.

Sparks re-entered the room. "Sorry that took so long. Maintenance opened up an old office and moved some things around so we can use it. Is your friend comin'?"

"Yeah. She should be here any minute."

Sparks walked in ahead of her and motioned for her to sit in one of the two metal chairs in front of the desk. Allison scanned the tiny room. It was the size of a standard walk-in closet, painted a dull gray, and boxes aligned the entire left wall. It was drab and isolated, mirroring Allison's own feelings. As David rounded the corner of the old metal desk a knock came at the door.

"Who is it," asked David Sparks?

The wooden door creaked open, exposing Sarah's profile. "Denise told me Allison is in here."

"Denise? Oh. Nurse Roberts. You must be Sarah…?"

"Yes sir, Sarah Buckman."

"Come on in and have a seat. Your friend is about to tell me the whole story of what happened tonight."

Sarah nodded, and then crossed the room to sit in the chair nearest the boxes. She wrapped her arm around Ali's shoulders. "Are ya ok hun?"

Ali's heart began beating faster. Her craving for a cigarette was getting even stronger. She did want Sarah there for moral support but was embarrassed to say what happened in front of her. She decided she was just going to have to bite the bullet and get it over with. She couldn't disinvite her now. Besides, Sarah wouldn't judge her.

Allison gazed up into Sarah's concerned face and said, "Well, after you left…I…was raped."

"Oh my God! Are you okay? Are ya hurt?" Sarah reached out and grabbed Ali's left hand as she sat down.

Having Sarah's full attention, plus, having her hand wrapped in Sarah's made Ali's heart pound harder. "Yeah, I'm ok. He didn't hurt me."

"Thank God," answered Sarah.

Sparks opened up his leather-bound notebook and got out a pen. "Alrighty then, so ya went to the bar, had a good time, your friend drove ya home, then what?"

Letting out a sigh to get up some gumption, Allison finally answered. "Well, I told ya I had been drinkin'...so Sarah helped me to the bedroom, took off my shoes, and set the alarm clock. Then, I guess I fell asleep because the next thing I know I couldn't move my arm; that's when I realized they were tied above my head." She looked down at the floor, hesitating. It was such an unbelievable story that she really couldn't be upset with either of them if they didn't believe her.

Noting her discomfort, Sparks attempted to relax her. "It's alright Ms. Carter, truly, there is nothin' you can tell me that I haven't heard before, and now your friend is here for support."

Sarah put her arm back around Allison's shoulders. "Darlin', you go right ahead. I'm here for ya." Sarah felt protective of Ali.

Ali looked at Sarah, gulped, and took a deep breath. Somehow having Sarah there was making things harder instead of easier. She scooted all the way back in her chair, crossed her arms, looked away from both of them, and started explaining the events of the evening. She could feel their eyes staring into her flesh.

"Well, at some point I heard a noise. I thought it was Casper, my cat, and that was when I couldn't move my arms. When I lifted my head I saw a dark figure at the foot of my bed. I tried to scream but nothing came out." A lonely tear drop made its way slowly down her cheek. She paused. Sarah reached out to her again, and squeezed her hand. Feeling safer, she finished. "He...he was pullin' the comforter and sheets off of me. I kicked my feet but it didn't seem to bother him. That made my dress ride up, and I wasn't wearin' panties."

Sarah let out a tiny gasp. Ali couldn't tell if it was excitement, shock, or intrigue. She suspected Sarah had a crush on her, but couldn't believe she'd be excited by her trauma, so she decided it was shock.

Looking back at Sparks, Ali continued, "Then he came over to the side of the bed. He was just standin' there lookin' down at my face and body. It was weird. Then his small hands reached under me to undo my dress. He pushed it up over my head, and then under my neck. I...I guess I was in shock or somethin', cause I stopped movin'. I...I didn't feel threatened, but I guess I should have. Then he exposed my boobs by undoin' the hook on the front of my bra."

Ali heard Sarah make the same little noise as before. She looked at Sarah but couldn't tell what the look on her face meant. Ali saw Sarah's chest heaving. Was she getting turned on by this, or upset?

"Please continue Ms. Carter," asked Sparks?

Returning her attention to Sparks, she answered, "Yes," with a small nod. "Well, then he put a finger on my neck and gently slid it down my body; startin' under my chin, then between my boobs, down to my navel, and then back up again. He climbed in bed with me. His knees were on either side of my hips. He bent down and kissed me passionately, but soft. He…licked my lips and moved down to my chest. It was more like…well, like he was making love to me!?" She said, in a confused voice. "I don't know and I sure don't understand, but that's when I saw his eyes. The lamp was on low, like normal, and his eyes were bright green peering through his mask."

Sarah slid her chair over to be directly beside Ali. She again wrapped her right arm around Ali's shoulders for comfort.

David Sparks adjusted his legs; they were aching. He easily ascertained that Sarah wanted to be more than just friends with Allison. They seemed to be in their own world. He thought of the two of them kissing, then immediately caught himself. "H-hm. So what happened next, ma'am?"

"Well, he licked me." She could tell by the look on Sparks' face that he needed more detail. Quickly, she blurted out, "He glided his tongue all around my boobs and stomach okay! It was like makin' love or somethin'. I've just never been made love to like that before. It's almost like it was meant for MY pleasure."

"Alright, I'm beginnin' to understand a little better," sighed Sparks.

"You...enjoyed...bein' made love to against your will," asked Sarah, with obvious confusion? She pulled Ali's head over on her shoulder and caressed her hair.

Ali popped her head up off of Sarah's shoulder. "Yes, okay...it didn't feel like rape...it was like a spiritual experience or somethin'."

Sparks looked down at the floor, searching for the words that should follow that statement.

Sarah slid her chair back to its original placement and stared wide-eyed at Ali.

Ali could see that Sparks was struggling for words, and that Sarah was intently trying to understand her. "Look, I'm tryin' to be honest here guys. I can't help how it made me feel. Oh my God! He even went down on me, and it was mind-blowin'! Right when I thought I was gonna cum, he stopped, unzipped his pants, then started you know, intercourse, but even that was slow and steady, just enjoyable; not like he was racin' to the finish line. After I had a vaginal orgasm he went down on me again! Oh God, my whole body was reactin', I couldn't stop it! I wanted to scream out, but not in fear. All my muscles were shakin', my eyes teared up, and...well...it felt like I peed on myself honestly. While I lay there all worn out, he casually got up, zipped his pants, kissed me good-bye, untied one wrist, then disappeared into the night. Look, I wouldn't have even come to the ER if I wasn't afraid I needed the mornin' after pill."

"Wow, you had one hell of a night, huh? You're sure this wasn't a dream? I mean you were pretty tipsy when I left." Sarah stroked the back of Ali's head.

Ali shook her head, and then looked at Sarah. "I wasn't that out of it. God! Why can't everybody just believe me?" She felt anger rising up inside her. She let out another frustrated sigh, and she could feel her eyes welling up with tears.

"Whoa! I didn't mean that I didn't believe ya. I'm just sayin' that you were pretty out of it when I left is all. I mean, I just want ya to be sure." She saw tears streaming down Ali's cheeks. She cupped Ali's face with the palm of her hand, and then wiped her tears away, using her thumb. She continued, in a crackly voice, "Ali I do believe ya. Ya know I'm always here for ya." Tears ran down Sarah's cheeks as well.

Ali too reached out to Sarah, cupping her face, and brushing her tears away. In Sarah's eyes she saw caring and compassion. "I know that. I didn't even think of callin' anybody other than you. You're my best friend, I knew you'd come for me." She grabbed Sarah's hand.

David Sparks watched the pair. The way they were staring into each other's eyes they were going to kiss at any moment. As a man he wanted to wait and see if they did, but as a cop he had to finish his job. "Sorry to interrupt this wonderful moment, but I need to know a bit more."

Both women sat up and looked at him.

"I already told ya everything," answered Ali.

"Ms. Carter, I need more of a description than green eyes and small hands. I mean, how tall was he? Did he have any visible scars or tattoos? Was he overweight, average, tall, short, or skinny? Oh, and the hard question. Is it possible that what you thought was a penis could have actually been a finger?"

Ali half-cocked her head up toward the ceiling and shook it. "I know what a dick feels like okay! Besides, his hands were on either side of my boobs while he was in and out of me."

"Calm down honey," Sarah suggested to Ali. She didn't like seeing Ali upset.

"Listen Ms. Carter I have to double check all the facts so that way we can find…"Mr. Loverboy." He didn't know what else to call him.

Ali's eyes were squinted, as she was thinking of what an asshole he was, but she was ready to get out of there so she cooperated. "Well, I think he was my height, but I was lying down remember?" Sarah was hanging on to her every word. "He was kinda small and light for guy really. I didn't notice any scars or tattoos but he was white, I think, well, his thing was. I mean the little lamp was on but it was on the lowest setting. I could make out some stuff, but not a lot."

"Okay, good. I need just one more thing from ya before ya go." He pushed a sheet of paper and a pen in front of her. "I need you to list every man that you've gone out with, had a one night stand with, rejected, and broken up with, over the last five years. 'Cause statistically, you know this man, well the chances are a lot higher anyways. At least fifty percent of crimes are committed against known subjects, because the perpetrators see a weakness, and they jump on it."

"Comforting," replied Ali, with a cynical tone. She wrote down four names then pushed them back to him. "Well, that's it for me. Can I go now?"

"Yeah. I'll be in touch, or if ya remember anything else please call me. You have my card. Thank ya for cooperatin', and please think about those groups, huh, they really might help ya." Sparks watched as they stood up, held each other's hand and exited the room.

"I really need a cigarette," said Ali.

"Well, you can smoke in the car."

"Thanks for comin' to get me. I know it's late."

"No problem honey," answered Sarah. She wrapped her arm around Ali's shoulders again.

As they approached the double doors that exited the emergency room, Ali's nurse waved goodbye to them and smiled politely. Ali waved sheepishly in her direction. Sarah smirked, and said, "Thanks for your help Denise."

2

Ali stared out the car window as the lights of the night blurred by. Her Newport was well worth the wait. She was thoroughly confused by the happenings of the night, and couldn't get her body to stop feeling excited.

Sarah broke the silence. "Okay ya little freak, tell me the truth, did ya really enjoy it?" She was secretly enthralled by her own thoughts.

They both erupted into giggles. As the giggles faded Ali cleared her throat. "Seriously?" Sarah nodded. "Yes! Oh my God! It was fuckin' awesome! I have never felt that way with ANY man before in my life. I mean, it was like this person knew exactly what to do and when. Ya know what I mean?" Ali was still in awe.

Sarah snickered. "Actually I do, that's how it is with us women, well, when you're in tune anyway."

"You mean sex can be like that all the time?" Ali was mystified.

Sarah smirked, and then calmly responded. "Yep, but like I said, only if you're in tune."

"Sarah I could swear I've been in tune with this guy before. Justin gave me an orgasm every time, just not like THAT."

"Hmm. Well I guess Mr. Loverboy knows how to do it better. Oh, by the way, it's called female ejaculation."

"Huh?" Ali had never heard that term.

"Ya know when ya felt like ya peed on yourself." Sarah glanced at Ali to see her physical response.

"Oh? I've never heard of that before." She only knew it was the best feeling she'd ever had. "I don't remember even mentioning that." She wondered how Sarah could possibly know what she had experienced. Her cheeks turned rosy red as she blushed, and she looked down at the floorboard of the car.

"Oh yeah!" Sarah thought of her own involvements with it. "Women all over the world try to do that, like every time they have sex, but it's rare. You should feel so lucky." Sarah had experienced it only a few times. She smiled to herself.

Awkwardly, Ali asked, "Well…have you ever, done that before?"

Sarah smiled. "Yeah I have. It's the best feelin' in the world. When I've done it my eyes water too."

"Mmm. I just can't get over it. Who did it to you?"

"Ali we've never talked about my sex life before. I've pretty much kept that from ya, on purpose, ya know, 'cause I'm a lesbian, and I never wanted to make you feel uncomfortable."

"Well, you don't have to anymore. I can handle it now…so…who was it?" Ali's interest was piqued. She wanted to do it again. She wondered why Sarah assumed she would be uncomfortable about two women having sex.

"The first one was Krista, this girl I used to work with. I was so embarrassed that I almost cried."

"Why?"

"I thought I peed in her face, and that was so not cool, but she loved it. She even laughed at me for gettin' upset."

Ali snickered. "Well how is it done? I mean, how does it work?"

Sarah sneered. "Are you sure you want me to tell you?"

"Yes!"

"Well…I go for the erogenous zones to make sure that the girl is good and wet." Sarah was a little hesitant with that information.

"I thought the "man in the boat" was the erogenous zone."

"Naw girly. That's the clit. When somebody really wants to please you they'll find the right spot, but it usually takes a few times to find it, so I guess Mr. Loverboy got lucky, and…so did you."

"Wait! How could a total stranger do that to me but not one single guy I've ever been with could?" Ali was perplexed.

"I…don't know," answered Sarah. She wondered the same thing.

"Do ya really think it could've been one of my exes?" Ali furled her eyebrows again.

Sarah giggled. When she glanced at Ali she saw her serious face. The giggle stopped immediately. "Oh, you're serious?" Her eyes shifted back and forth. She didn't have all the answers. She wished she did. "Honey…I have no idea, I mean, I guess it's possible. Anything is possible, but…why didn't they do that to ya when ya'll were together?"

"Good point. Um, maybe they learned some new skills since we broke up." Ali was trying to figure out who it could have been.

"But then, why not ring the doorbell, instead of showin' up in the middle of the night with a mask on?" She was trying to make Ali think logically.

Her condescending tone irritated Ali, so with attitude, she retorted, "Uh, maybe because they know I don't give second chances."

Sarah seemed shocked. "Wha…really?"

"Yeah. Not all of us are hopeless romantics. I mean why do ya do that Sarah – just let somebody screw ya over time and again? I mean, are ya a glutton for punishment or what?" Why set yourself up for heartbreak all over again?

"Unbelievable," Sarah muttered. No wonder she has issues with love.

"Why? Huh? 'Cause I would be a fool to take somebody back that had already screwed up. I mean, obviously their not the one for me." She flicked her cigarette out the window, but left it cracked.

"Wow! I didn't realize you were so cold and blind Ali." Sarah's mind was running rampant with reasons to go back out with someone a second time.

"What the hell are you talking about?" How dare Sarah talk about her that way?

Sarah knew she'd struck a nerve but couldn't seem to stop her mouth from moving. "Everybody deserves a second chance."

Ali cocked an eyebrow up, as if to say she was out of her mind.

Sarah continued, "No, seriously, think about it this way. There are two parts to every relationship; physical and emotional. If you have good physical chemistry but not emotional it ends up just bein' sex, which gets old after a while, but if you have a good emotional bond you can work on the physical aspect. I mean, maybe they just don't have the skills you'd like for 'em to have, but that can be fixed. Either you decide the bond is worth bad sex or ya try to train 'em with what ya like, so you can have both. That's the goal for everybody, ya know, to have both."

"Well yeah, but…goin' back to somebody who already messed up is redundant, isn't it"? Ali couldn't see any other way to look at it.

Sarah sighed. How could she open Ali's eyes? She thought for a moment, and then replied. "Let's say ya run into an ex two years down the road and ya know ya have one aspect, you can still feel it, and its strong, wouldn't it be worth the effort to see if the person had grown into the ONE that can give ya both?"

"Not when the first time around it was only sex."

"Yeah but what about if the one ya run into was an emotional spark? Then what? Huh? Half of sex is skill. What if their skills have gotten better? Most do with time." Sarah was determined to get her point across.

"Sarah just leave it alone. Either way it would be takin' a step backwards, and I don't want to do that."

"How is it goin' backwards? Don't YOU change as you grow?"

"Of course I do."

"Then how come ya don't think others can change as they grow? Huh? Ali, can ya honestly tell me that if ya knew your ex had changed and could possibly give ya both aspects of a good relationship that ya wouldn't give him a chance to prove it? I mean, ugh, they could be the great love of your life, your soul mate, and you'd just brush 'em off cause he couldn't do it in the past? That's so…selfish…and…self-deprivin'."

Ali looked down at the floor board, dumb-founded. After several minutes had passed she calmly said, "Well if I knew that they'd really changed…I might give 'em a second chance." She was surprised by her own answer. She turned to face the car window so Sarah couldn't see that she was full of self-doubt.

Sarah smirked in amusement at her small victory. "I think it's your view of love that keeps any of your relationships from lastin'."

Ali yanked her head around to look at Sarah. "So all of my failed relationships are my fault?"

"Well…kinda."

"HOW?" Ali couldn't believe Sarah would say that.

Sarah knew she'd really gotten under Ali's skin, and felt compelled to finish her thought. "It's just that ya look at love through tunnel vision."

"What the hell is that supposed to mean?" Ali was confused.

"Okay. To you, let's say…love is an oval. You ignore the circles, squares, triangles, rectangles, and stars, because in your head an oval is the best match for ya. BUT, but, what you're actually doin'…is limitin' yourself 'cause you end up missin' out on what all the other shapes have to offer. I mean what if a square is your true soul mate and ya spend your whole life lookin' for an oval? You're never gonna be as happy as you could be." She saw Ali's face softening into thought.

"So, what am I supposed to do?" Ali was feeling uncomfortable.

"Baby, ya gotta open yourself up to love. Stop tryin' to control how ya feel. Let it come to ya naturally. Ya know, go with the flow. True, actual, real love is unconditional. That is why I give second chances. See, love changes as it grows; that's normal. But ya have to be open to it. If ya keep goin' like ya are, you're gonna end up bein' a lonely forty-year old who just settles for one-night stands."

"Hey! One night stands can be good."

"Sure if all ya want is sex. But we both know women want more than that. We want a connection. Love is about give and take, compromise and risk. If you're not riskin' anything, or willin' to compromise, then ya don't really want anyone in your life, and we both know that's not true or you woulda quit tryin' by now…I just don't want ya to be lonely and unhappy okay?"

As the car stopped Ali quickly threw her arms around Sarah's neck and cried into her silky brown hair.

"What's this," asked Sarah? "I just told you that out of love and concern." She slowly rubbed Ali's back. She could feel Ali's bra and felt no clasp. She shuddered at the thought of Ali's boobs pressing against her own. She imagined for a second that she was opening the hooks in the front of her bra.

Ali cleared her throat. "I know you're just concerned." She looked up into Sarah's eyes, and continued, "Nobody gets me like you do."

Sarah gulped. She could see Ali's eyes were swollen, and her cheeks glistened as cars drove by. As she beheld Allison's eyes she could think only of their lips touching. She moistened her own lips with her craving tongue. Even in the darkness she could see Ali's caramel-brown eyes piercing her, to her very core. She felt as though all the oxygen in the car had evaporated. The only sounds were their breathing, and her heartbeat.

"You're the best friend that I've ever had," resumed Ali.

Softly the radio was playing Sophie B. Hawkins' *Damn I Wish I Was Your Lover*.

Sarah couldn't stop the tears that were streaming down her face. They hit the rim of her tank top before she even realized she was crying. She was obviously stuck in the "friend zone" with Ali, and always would be. She swiftly wiped her face, neck, and chin. She had been crushing on Ali since the first time she saw her, but now it had developed into love. The harsh realization that it would never evolve into a romantic relationship was over-whelming. She was experiencing a brokenness she didn't expect. She'd wanted to tell Ali about how she truly felt but was too scared that she'd lose her completely, and now was definitely not the time to talk about it. She decided to wait until Ali was less stressed. In the meantime she would just pick up on her duties as best friend.

"Hey. Where are you?" Ali noticed that Sarah was quiet and crying.

"Huh?" Ali's voice pulled her out of her own head.

"Well you were lookin' down at the steerin' wheel and not answerin' me," Ali replied.

Sarah took a deep breath. The intensity of her emotions were hard to swallow. She closed her eyes and concentrated on what she should say, and not what she wanted to say. She cleared her throat, and then said, "Sorry, I guess I'm gettin' tired Hun."

"Oh, well no wonder. Look at the time." She pointed to the CD player. It read 3:49.

"Aw man! Oh well. Tomorrow is a half day. I can sleep when I get off work." Sarah was willing to lose a little sleep if it meant she would be able to spend time with Ali.

Ali looked out her window. Her house looked the same yet different. "Will ya still come get me in the mornin' before work or ya just wanna wait to get my car until after work?"

"Whoa!" Sarah threw her hand in the air. "You still wanna go to work?" She thought Ali was being too passive about the events of the evening.

Furrowing her eyebrows at Sarah, Ali answered, "Well yeah, why not? It's not like I'm hurt or anything."

Sarah responded by sucking her teeth and saying, "Hmm, maybe because you just got raped!?"

"Attitude!" Ali scolded Sarah for what seemed like back talk to her.

Sarah smiled coyly. "What? So...it didn't affect you? You're invincible? Cause I gotta tell ya...ya been starin' at your house like ya don't even recognize it...okay, 'Ms. Everything is Fine.' Why haven't ya got out of the car yet?" Sarah was afraid Ali was pushing herself too fast.

A long, quiet minute passed. "I liked it, don't ya get it? What if he comes back? What if...I...want him...to...come back? Doesn't that make me like bad, or weird, or wrong, or somethin'?" Sharing her guilt with Sarah seemed to take some of its power away.

"So...you're afraid to go back in there because...he might come back? Well, first of all, you didn't do anything wrong, so ya shouldn't be hangin' your head in shame. Second, ya can't help what ya like, any more than the rest of the human race. And third, sittin' out here at 3:51 a.m. isn't gonna change your feelin's. You're entitled to 'em, and I'm sorry, but they're gonna be there no matter where ya are." She was trying to encourage Ali.

"I know, I know. I just don't feel like I was really raped. It was beautiful, tender, and...perfect."

"Okay Ali darlin, then why are you fightin' it so hard? Why don't ya just go on in?" Sarah's eyebrows rose toward her hairline.

"I guess, because...it makes me feel dirty, for likin' it." Ali's shoulders dropped as she confessed this. She looked down at the floorboard of the SUV. If she liked it now, did she like it as a child when her uncle would do the same things to her? Is that why she liked it? She was thoroughly confused about how to feel. She only knew it exhilarated her.

Through a chuckle, Sarah inquired, "Ok. So ya gonna go in, shower, and wait for him to come back?"

Slyly, Ali cocked an eyebrow, smiled, and then said, "Hmm, maybe." What was she going to do?

"Ha-ha. Seriously though. Are you okay?" Sleepiness was settling in on Sarah and she wanted to make sure Ali was alright before she left her to her own devices.

"Yeah. Of course. I have a question for you though Ms. Thang." Ali bobbed her head back and forth.

"Oh Lord. What is it?" Sarah was truly wondering what was on Ali's mind.

"Well, at the hospital, ya called the nurse by her first name. How do ya know her?"

Sarah blushed. "It's a long story babe." She wanted to skip the subject.

"I have time." Ali was more curious now.

"Nah. You only think ya wanna know. It's nothin', really." Sarah tried to deter her.

"No, really…please tell me." Ali poked out her bottom lip and batted her eyelashes at Sarah.

"Right now is really an inappropriate time for it."

"Come on Sarah. I'm not getting' out until ya tell me." Ali felt giddy inside.

"Fine!" She couldn't seem to say no to Ali. "Well, I'd seen her in a bar in Atlanta and hit on her. She was there with her husband, who came walkin' up at that moment. I was embarrassed. Then a couple of months later I saw her here in town. She was alone so we talked. We fooled around once. Ok? Happy?"

Ali could tell she'd left something out. "Wait a minute. What really happened, and I want all the details." She felt captivated by the thought of Sarah "fooling around" and wanted a visual.

Sarah paused. "Well…I knew she was a nurse, but she used to work at Dr. Haney's office, the skin doctor. I made myself an appointment because I had a patch of dry skin, and because I knew she'd be there. Well when I got to my appointment sure enough, there she was, lookin' fine as usual. I waited in the room for about twenty minutes. The doctor came in, looked at me, and gave me a prescription. He told me the nurse would be right with me to explain what to do with the cream… I've got chills just thinkin about it."

Ali was anxious. "Well what? Tell me, please."

"Ok! Geez. You know this ain't up your alley, right?" Pretending to discourage women's interest in lesbian sex had worked for her in the past, when it came to making a woman more interested in her.

"Ok, just tell me already!" Ali really wanted the details.

"Alright…well, she came in and asked me if I was attracted to her, without even sayin' hello or anything. I hesitantly said yeah. Then she locked the door. My heart started poundin' right away. I had no idea what was about to happen. So she walks over to me, runs her fingers through my hair and tells me she wants to kiss me. I asked about her husband. She said she wouldn't tell him if I didn't. That turned me on bigger than shit. I mean just the thought of doin' somethin' on the down low, ya know? Anyhow…so she bends down and kisses me. And she's a damn good kisser. Then she starts rubbing my nipples. I reach up and pull her down on my lap so she's straddlin' my legs. I had my hand in her scrub top, pinching her little boobs, and then I just slid my hand down into her bottoms, without even thinkin' about it…I fingered her. She was yellin' into my neck and bitin' it. I guess so no one else could hear her. After she was done ridin' my hand she got up, took some deep breaths, fixed her clothes, kinda tossed my hair with her fingers, then said 'Mmmm', and left the room."

"Oh my God. That's so sexy, I can't believe it." Ali was turned on. Her breaths were coming faster.

"Yeah it was hard for me to believe it too, and to look at her after that. I mean I left the office in shock. I told the office ladies to have a good day and she came around the corner sayin' she was already havin' a good day. I left.

Ever since then, when I see her, I realize she just wanted an experience, and that she used me. But I'll tell ya what, I was so turned on, if I had balls they would've been blue, plus I had a hickey for like two weeks."

Ali was a little jealous. Had Sarah ever been turned on by her? She stared at her house. It looked like its boring old self again. She didn't want her time with Sarah to end.

Sarah sensed Ali was not going to get out of the car. "I could sleep over if ya want. That couch of yours is pretty comfy."

"Sarah Ravenal Buckman!"

Sarah was stunned. "What Allison VERONICA Carter?"

"You are too good to me. You don't have to sleep on the couch. Hell, I have a California King, there's more than enough room for ya in the bed. By the way…what shape are you?"

Sarah smiled, and then confidently spoke. "Oh…I'm a star baby."

Ali smiled, admiring Sarah's bold statement. "I'm not sure what I am yet."

"Well, you're only twenty-eight. You've got plenty of time to figure it out. Anyhow, I was serious about stayin', if ya need me to." She wanted to get closer to Ali.

Ali smiled. "Thanks, and you act like thirty-six is so old." She felt as if her body was a huge pile of fireworks that just needed a spark.

"Honey please, and you're more than welcome." Sarah smiled on the outside, keeping up appearances. On the inside she was struggling with staying with Ali, or leaving her. Either way she would be tortured in one way or another.

Ali let out a deep breath, opened the passenger side door, and then put one foot on the curb. She turned back to Sarah and said, "Well...are ya comin' or what?" She was afraid to go into her home alone. The guilty pleasure of her experience was overrunning her senses.

Sarah's heart sped up. "Uh, yeah, ok. Let me just go home and get some clothes right quick."

"Why? I'm sure I have somethin' you can wear, plus I have a brand new pack of panties, never been opened."

With a light, nervous chuckle Sarah said, "Hmm, alright, well then, let's...go in." Sarah had fantasized about sleeping with Ali for a long time but the circumstances weren't what she desired. She was going to step into the role of best friend, but wouldn't mind catching a peek of her in the shower, if the occasion arose.

The dark night and street lights cast shadows on the lawn, but there was enough light for Sarah to watch the way that Ali's hips swayed back and forth, as she had done a thousand times before. This time seemed different though.

Her movement was more exaggerated. Sarah wondered if Ali was doing this just for her, or if she even realized she was doing it.

3

The house was quiet. The bedroom light had been left on. Ali walked slowly through the dark kitchen, and into the bedroom. Sarah followed. Ali began going through her chest of drawers.

"Here, told ya, plenty to choose from. Uh…could ya do me a favor? Could ya feed Casper? And please, make yourself at home. I'm gonna hop in the shower." She felt as though a shower would wash away some of the guilt she felt for liking the rape.

Sarah nodded. "No prob Bob. Thanks for the clothes." Sarah wanted to keep the mood light.

She was definitely in the "friend zone" now. She watched as the bathroom door closed tightly behind Ali, but didn't hear it lock. This had her plotting to go in while she was showering. She quickly went to the kitchen cabinets. Finding the cat food was easy. She'd been there several times and had seen Ali feed the cat before. She opened a small can of wet cat food and Casper appeared out of nowhere. He rubbed his furry white tail across Sarah's leg. Sympathetically, she said, "I know Mr. Casper Kitty. I've got somethin' you want." She laughed at herself for talking to him like a baby. She strained to hear if the shower was running yet, but all she could hear was Casper's purring. After scraping the contents of the can into the pet dish, Sarah rinsed off the spoon, and then flipped off the light on her way into the bedroom.

On the foot of the giant bed was a tiny pile of clothes. Ali had laid them there for Sarah's use. Out of curiosity, she picked up the new pack of panties first. She often wondered what type of panties Ali wore. She was surprised. Instead of the lace-lined, silky, hi-cuts she expected, she saw female boxers. They were one-hundred percent cotton; no lace anywhere. Sarah opened the pack and pulled out the black pair. She preferred them to the navy blue and hunter green. The squeal of the water coursing through the pipes, and running into the shower got her attention. She was titillated by the thought that Ali was standing naked, just six feet away, on the other side of the door. Her mind was running wild with ideas, all sexual. She shook her head and reminded herself she was there as Ali's friend. She turned her head away from the direction of the bathroom and back to the bed. She stared at the spot where she imagined Ali was laying as she was raped. The shower curtain slid across the metal rod and Sarah knew she had a limited time to snoop. She just had to know if Ali wore sexy underwear. She walked to the oak chest of drawers and opened the top drawer, as she'd seen Ali do. To her delight there was a cornucopia of thongs, hi-cuts, briefs, boxers, and lace undergarments, of all colors. A contented smile spread across her face. She slowly and quietly closed the drawer. Sarah turned and faced the bed again. She deducted that changing the bed sheets may be beneficial to Ali, so she stripped them off and threw them in the washing machine. She then rummaged through the hall closet until she found more sheets and changed the bed. She went to the kitchen to get a glass of water; anything to take her mind off of a naked Ali. She got some sweet iced tea instead. She briskly returned to the bedroom. She positioned herself at the foot of the bed, across from the bathroom door. She hoped Ali would forget she was there and come out naked. The water turned off and she jumped backwards toward the headboard, hitting her head. "Ow", she whispered, as she rubbed the back of her head. She couldn't decide which way she should be laying or sitting when Ali opened the door, and tried several angles. This made her giggle because she'd seen this before, in movies, but now she understood the reasoning behind it. She settled for sitting on the side of the bed, holding her glass of iced tea. She thought of rushing into the bathroom while Ali was still exposed, but was satisfied with the inside glimpse she'd already received into Ali's personal life. She thought of how this night would change their working relationship. They'd be closer she suspected.

They had worked together for two and a half years, but had only really gotten close over the last six months;

since they'd both ended relationships. Their closeness was derived from meeting a few of the girls from the bank every Tuesday night, and they'd somehow ended up hanging out mostly with each other. Perhaps it was because they were the only two that were single. Sarah had been attracted to her for two years. That attraction turned to love over the last half year, but Allison was a special creature; one to be worshipped not ogled, or sexualized. Sarah's gay friends often picked at her for trying to turn the "straightest" girls gay, or at least bi-sexual. There are already so many stereotypes about homosexuals that she thought her gay and lesbian friends should have a little more respect for the issue. Many of her fellow Georgians held firm beliefs in the stereotypes that all gay people sleep around with anyone of the same sex, and that they're always trying to make more gay people, that they molest kids, and that they all do drugs. How ridiculous. Those are a few of the reasons why some people feel like they have to hide who they truly are, and end up living in unfulfilling or unloving romantic relationships. At least our society is finally becoming more educated about the myths surrounding gays…The squeak of the bathroom door diverted her train of thought. Ali's eyes were still a little swollen. She looked sleepy.

"Well, do ya feel any better hun," asked Sarah, with hope in her eyes?

"Yeah, I guess so." Ali shrugged her shoulders.

Sarah wasn't convinced. "What's wrong baby?"

"Oh, it's nothin'."

"Ali, if somethin' is wrong, I'm right here." Sarah hoped she was going to tell her that she wanted a kiss or something. "Are you afraid it'll embarrass me or somethin', cause I don't embarrass easily…one time I was even dared to run down the road naked, in broad daylight, and I did it, of course I was seventeen at the time, but anyhow…" Why did she tell her that?

Ali was intrigued by that statement. The thought of Sarah running naked down the road made Ali's face flush a rose color. "That would have been somethin' to see, but no, that's not really it. It's just that, well, I haven't wanted anyone in my bed since Justin left, and now I'll have two in one night."

Sarah was excited that Ali slipped up and said she wanted to see her naked but let down by the fact that she didn't want her in her bed. "Ali, honey, I can leave. I don't have to stay. I mean, it was your idea."

"No, you misunderstood! I don't want you to leave, I just… um…" Ali looked down with uncertainty.

Ali's dirty blonde hair was still wet. It appeared brown, almost as dark as Sarah's. There was a natural body to it that she'd never noticed before. The kiss of the sun was evident in her beautiful golden brown skin, all year long. Her father was Mexican. Water was glistening on the sides of her neck. Her robe was made of red silk, and clinging to her semi-moist skin, as well as exposing her from her thighs to her bare feet.

"Honey, I don't know what ya want me to do. If ya want me to stay I can sleep on the couch. That's what I offered to start with." Tears welled up in Ali's eyes, reminding Sarah of how vulnerable she was at the moment. "It's okay baby. I know you're upset right now, and it's been a long night. We're cool okay." She stood up, walked to Ali, and hugged her. She whispered in her ear, "Why don't you get some sleep?"

Ali felt she needed to vindicate herself, and spoke into Sarah's neck. "I didn't mean anything personal, I swear. I don't really think you're gonna try to sleep with me just 'cause you're a lesbian."

With a nervous guffaw, Sarah stepped away from Ali. The heat of Ali's breath had sent shivers down Sarah's body, causing her nipples to harden, and after that statement she didn't want Ali to feel them. She smiled innocently at Ali.

"The truth is you've never looked at me like that have you Sarah?" Ali was feeling confused again. She wanted Sarah to long for her, but she was afraid of her.

Sarah had a sinking feeling in the pit of her stomach. If she answered truthfully, her secret would be brought to light. Plus, what if Ali just wanted to experiment with her? She'd be left heart broken. She wouldn't be able to stand it if that's what happened between the two of them. She deeply cared for her, but her view of Ali was slowly rupturing. She always felt vulnerable around Ali, but never more than this one particular moment.

"What exactly are ya asking Ali?" She crossed her arms and prepared to be let down, yet again.

"Okay, please stop lookin' at me like that! Honestly? I've never been this close to a woman before, and especially not a lesbian!"

"Uh-huh, and would we even be havin' this conversation if I was one of your straight friends?" Sarah picked up her clothes from the foot of the bed, walked around Ali without looking at her, and disappeared into the bathroom.

Ali slumped down on the bed, banging her head against the headboard. She immediately jerked up to a sitting position and rubbed the crown of her head. She thought of Sarah. The physical bump was much like the point Sarah had just made; it stung. She was so stressed over her feelings for Sarah that she just didn't know how to be anymore, or what to say. She could only imagine that she'd never get to explore those feelings now, and after that story about the nurse she didn't want to be one of those girls. She lit a Newport and tried to relax.

Sarah ran a warm bubble bath and settled in to relax. She looked around at the shampoo, conditioner, and body washes. She smelled them. Sarah knew why Ali smelled so good. She thought how obvious it was that Ali had bought into some of the stereotypes about lesbians.

Next she'll be asking if I've slept with all my lesbian friends, if I was molested as a kid, and if not, what turned me gay. She scoffed cynically at the thought. This was not the same person who she'd gotten to know so well. She figured tonight was just different because she was under stress, but thinking back over the last few weeks, Ali had asked some pretty colorful questions. What was going on with her lately? Sarah's anger dissipated as she thought of the fact that no one can go back in time and change how they were brought up to think. A knock came at the door.

"Yeah," answered Sarah.

"I'm really sorry Sarah." Ali couldn't fathom not talking to her anymore, and she had an uncontrollable urge to see her naked.

"It's alright. I'm not mad." How could she be mad at Ali?

"Do ya mind if I grab my toothbrush? I can go to the guest bathroom and brush my teeth."

Sarah sighed and shook her head. Calmly, she answered, "This is your bathroom, in your house. You can do whatever ya want to."

"Well I don't want to disturb ya or anything." She wanted Sarah to want her to come in.

An amused smirk spread across Sarah's face. "Just come on in!"

Ali entered the bathroom. She could see that Sarah was covered by bubbles, but still couldn't resist looking at her.

Sarah noticed Ali's eyes darting back and forth, from her, and then back to her own image in the mirror. She became aroused. Her nipples hardened and a warm thumping began between her legs. She twitched involuntarily, as her muscles began doing kegels. Sarah wanted to reach down and massage her clitoris, but she wouldn't dare do that with Ali in the room. She could feel Ali's eyes on her bare flesh and her body grew warmer with each glance. Her body was aching for satisfaction, yet she welcomed the intrusion. She'd slid down in the tub from the movement, so she re-adjusted. This time she made sure her nipples emerged from the water. Then she stared at the mirror and waited for Ali to look her way again.

Ali bent over to spit out her toothpaste. She wondered if Sarah was checking out her butt. As her head came back up she glanced in the mirror again. Sarah's nicely rounded D-cups and hard nipples were staring back at her, as was Sarah. Her groin instantly moistened with a warm discharge. She gasped and quickly returned her eyes to her own reflection.

Slyly, Sarah asked, "What's the matter darlin'?"

"Oh, I'm just, nothin', gotta pee!" She slammed her toothbrush down and scurried out of the bathroom.

Sarah smiled, thinking there may be hope for them yet. She then pleasured her tormented body with the vision of Ali's eyes on her. She came almost immediately. She readied herself for spending the night with Ali. That thought made the thumping return, hidden away, in her black boxers.

Sarah strutted out of the bathroom and Ali wasn't in the bedroom. She went looking for her and saw the light coming from beneath the guest bathroom door, in the dark hallway. She heard heavy breathing and panting. Inside she suddenly felt bouncy and giggly. She thrust her fists in the air as if she'd won an Academy Award. Her emotions were over-taking her again. The bellow of laughter in her gut was trying to surface, luckily only a tiny squeak escaped her teeth. The heavy breathing stopped abruptly. Sarah turned and scampered off, back to the master bedroom, quietly.

Ali washed her hands. She peered at herself in the mirror. She knew now that she was attracted to Sarah, which confused her even more, because she'd never actually wanted to kiss or touch another female before. A memory of Sarah's half-naked body flashed to the forefront of her mind. Her clitoris was still sensitive, even to thought, plus, she was right at the cusp of an orgasm when she'd heard a noise. She hoped it was Casper. If it was Sarah she'd never be able to look her in the eyes again. Slowly, she opened the door and peeked out. Casper was sitting in front of the door looking up at her. "Whew!" She bent over, stroked Casper, and then walked back to the bedroom. Sarah was squatting in front of the bathroom door, searching for something under the sink.

"Hey Sarah, what are ya lookin' for?"

"Toothbrush", Sarah answered, without looking up.

Ali walked over, squatted beside her, pointed to a medium-sized make-up bag, and said, "In there."

"Thanks," Sarah said, breathing in the mixture of Ali's shampoo and fresh musk scent smell, and it was incredible.

"You're welcome."

Ali turned and walked back over to the bed. She took off her robe and pulled the comforter back. She realized the bed was made and had clean sheets on it. She looked around questioningly, and then threw her robe across the arm of the rocking chair near the bed. The sound of Sarah brushing her teeth turned her head toward the bathroom. She watched as toned bicep and buttock muscles flexed with Sarah's every move. She was very feminine for a dikey lesbian; her toenails were even polished, bright rose. She was quite sexy. Of course the power suits that she wore to work didn't show this side of her, but Ali's eyes were open to it now. Sarah had high cheek bones, intense hazel blue eyes, adorable dimples, a beautiful smile, a toned body, and the softest brown hair with a hint of auburn streaks, but only when the light hit it just right. Ali wondered exactly what her ancestry was; maybe Native American. The boxers were fitted to her muscular thighs. The contrast of the white tank top on her skin enunciated her cinnamon colored arms. Casper brushed against Ali's leg. "Oh shit!" She looked down and was relieved to see Casper. By the time she looked back up Sarah was by her side.

"Are you okay baby?"

"Yeah", Ali answered through a nervous chuckle. "I, uh, just felt somethin' on my leg, it scared me is all... Uh...why do you always call me pet names?"

"Huh?" Sarah didn't understand the question.

"Ya know, baby, honey, darlin', sweetie." Ali's head bobbed, from side to side, with each name.

Sarah was baffled. She opened her mouth to speak but no words came out. She cleared her throat. "Well, it's not just you, is it? I mean, I do that to everybody, right? I, uh, really don't know why."

"Oh...okay," Ali said with discernible disappointment. She wanted Sarah to treat only her with special attention.

Intuitively, Sarah responded jokingly. "Well I can try to stop if you want me to."

"What? No, that's not what I meant, I just, I don't know. Boyfriends have called me pet names..."

They stared at each other. The sexual tension couldn't have been cut with a chainsaw. Sarah was now certain Ali wanted more, but how much more? She was apprehensive. She didn't want to get hurt or lose Ali all together.

An uncontrollable urge kept resonating within Ali. She wanted to kiss Sarah, badly, but was afraid. She looked down at the floor then back up at Sarah's plump inviting lips. Her breathing became erratic. She thought the moment would pass her by if she didn't take it, and who knows if she'd ever get the chance again. "Sarah…I, uh," her voice became shaky. "I have noticed a big change, in myself, over the last couple of months or so…it's because of…well, my feelings have changed…for…you." She paused, drinking in the puzzled look on Sarah's face, but had to finish her thought. "It has never been as powerful, though, as it is tonight."

Sarah was unsure of how to respond. Did Ali only want her for one night, or did she just realize it on this night? Did she want an attempt at a relationship? Is she just saying this because she's horny right now, actually into her, or just still reeling from the rape? With a sad tone Sarah asked, "Just tonight?"

"No! I don't think so. I just know I really wanna kiss you, and I've never wanted to kiss a woman before, but…there's just somethin' about you, that I can't put my finger on…that gets to me." She stared into Sarah's eyes, feeling as though she couldn't look away, as if she were melting into Sarah.

Sarah was satisfied with Ali's words. They were honest, and a kiss denotes intimacy, not just a one night stand. "I have plenty you can put your finger on, but let's take it slow."

A relieved smile passed Ali's cheeks. "So you do feel the same way about me?"

"Yeah; for a while now. Don't sound so surprised." Sarah wanted to boost Ali's confidence.

"But I...don't know how to be with a woman. You might be disappointed."

"Never baby. I didn't know at first either. You just have to go with what feels right and let nature take its course. There's plenty of time to..."

Ali reached out and pulled Sarah down to her, and kissed her passionately. Their tongues spun around each other's ferociously. They both moaned in an ecstatic state, while their hands molested each other's backs, hair, and breasts. Ali slid her hand inside Sarah's tank top. Sarah pulled away.

"You didn't do anything wrong Ali. I just want to make sure we save somethin' for another time. We don't have to rush."

"You're the best kisser ever!"

Sarah smiled. "You're pretty damn good yourself."

"Ok...so can we kiss more if I promise not to touch you?"

Sarah looked bewildered. "It's not that I don't want you to touch me baby. I do, really bad, but I want to make sure it's not too over-whelmin' to you. Neither of us wants to get hurt, and I'm afraid if we move too fast…we will."

"I'm sorry. I don't know what came over me." Ali was still breathing heavy. She licked her lips, tasting Sarah on them.

"Oh trust me baby, I know exactly what it is."

Ali licked her lips. "Oh God! I want you to kiss me some more. I've got chills all over, and my panties are wet again, even though…well I've got a steady pulse down there."

"Mmmm. Mine is pulsin' too."

Ali gasped in titillation, then quickly stepped up to Sarah and meshed their bodies together. Their mouths met with familiarity and fire. Ali's hands slid down Sarah's back, to her buttocks. She squeezed them then pulled Sarah closer to her.

Again Sarah distanced herself. "Whoa! We have got to slow down. Why don't we…um…go to sleep?"

Ali appeared hurt. She rolled her eyes. "Whatever."

"Do you like to snuggle? I do. Look, I just don't want to, um, you were just raped! I mean, I don't want you to feel like I took advantage of ya, and I don't know that ya aren't just turned on cause of him."

"No, Sarah, it's definitely you. I understand though, so yeah, let's do it. Let's go to sleep together." She didn't want to send Sarah mixed messages, but she really did want to do more than kiss. Ali stepped out on the back deck in her shorts and tank top to smoke.

As she stood there her mind wandered. She was guessing that sex with Sarah would be great, but she was afraid to touch her down there. She wasn't sure of what to do, but she sure did want to try, and especially wanted to kiss her some more. She was anticipating an excruciatingly tortured night's sleep lying next to her and only snuggling.

4

The warmth of Sarah's body was fantastic. Ali felt very secure next to her. Per usual, Ali had woken up before the alarm clock went off, but she was happy about it today. Sarah was snuggled up to her back, and had her right arm wrapped around her waist all night. Spooning with Sarah was incredible; she'd never liked it so much with her boyfriends. It was as if their bodies were made for cuddling with each other. She was careful not to wake Sarah because she didn't want her to move. Her thoughts were filled with what she could do to prove that she wanted more than just a physical relationship with Sarah, but she was so curious for her that she couldn't stand it anymore; she had to touch her. Ali reached around behind her, placing her hand on Sarah's hip. She began rubbing her from hip to knee. A soft moan came from Sarah, and she twitched. Ali moved her hand to the back of Sarah's leg. She caressed from the top of her thigh to her buttocks. Sarah moaned louder and her pelvic region humped into Ali's buttocks, very calmly.

"Mmmm," Sarah mumbled. Now Ali's body was twitching. Sarah ran her hand up and over Ali's shoulder, then down her back, and across her buttocks. Ali gasped. Sarah's touch was so sweet and meaningful, yet stimulating. Ali was turned on again. She leaned back into Sarah, threw her arm back on her hip, and caressed it again.

Sarah nuzzled her nose into Ali's neck and whispered, "Good mornin' Beautiful".

Sarah's breath on her neck sent shivers all over Ali's body, and she moaned aloud.

"Mmmm," Sarah mumbled again.

Ali turned over on her back. Sarah leaned down and kissed her. Ali's internal temperature was rising, which made her hips writhe up and down.

Sarah smiled. She was elated that Ali was turned on by her. She used her middle finger to trace the outline of Ali's nipples, which made them both breathe heavily. Their emotions came through in the constant fiery kisses they shared. Sarah slid her hand down Ali's stomach and across the top of her cotton boxers. Ali breathed loudly. Sarah looked into her eyes. They were saying, "It's all yours." Sarah wanted to ravage Ali's body in a sensual way. She was so turned on she felt that she might explode. She licked Ali's neck, and then her lips. "I want to see you," Sarah said softly.

Ali stood up slowly and took off her tank top.

Sarah smiled and licked her lips. "I want to see more of you," she said playfully.

Shyly, Ali turned around and removed her boxers.

Sarah was in awe. Ali's body was perfect in her eyes; full cheeks, voluptuous curves, sandy blonde hair, adoring brown eyes, beautifully delicate hands, and long legs with thick thighs. "I so totally approve."

"You do, even though I have a flat butt?"

"Especially because of your curves...and your butt is cute. Will you turn around now?"

Ali turned her head, to peer at Sarah over her left shoulder. "What about you?"

"Not a problem for me." Sarah jumped up off the bed and stripped off her clothes. Then she walked up behind Ali. She wrapped her arms around her waist, then splayed kisses and licks all over her neck, back, and shoulder blades. She gently fondled Ali's thighs and buttocks, and then up to her ribs. Sarah turned Ali around and stopped to admire the view. "Oh baby, you are so beautiful." She slid her hand in between Ali's legs and sweetly touched her labia. Ali gasped and opened her legs wider. Sarah smirked then easily slid her middle finger just inside. She could feel Ali's clitoris jumping. She wiggled her digit the tiniest bit. Apparently this weakened Ali, because she stepped into Sarah, hard.

"Are you okay baby?" Sarah smiled. She was happy to be turning Ali on.

"Yeah...I just, well you went right to...Oh my God!" Ali's words were breathy.

"Is that a good oh my God?" Sarah was a playful lover.

"Mmm-hmm," she answered with conviction.

Sarah smirked again. She was pleased to be the one to take Ali on her journey into same-sex relationships. She helped Ali back to the bed, and then brushed her hair back out of her face. As her hand brushed by she could smell Ali on her finger; this sent chills throughout Sarah's body. Ali smelled delicious. She tenderly laid Ali down so that her legs were draped over the side of the bed. Sarah then straddled her. Ali looked up at Sarah with innocent anticipation. She rotated her vagina all over Ali's. Ali licked her lips and then reached up to play with Sarah's breasts. Ali began grinding against Sarah as well. They locked lips and tongues. She slowly backed down Ali's body with her legs, and then bent over to suckle her nipples, one at a time. Ali played with Sarah's hair. Sarah sucked Ali's nipples slightly harder; Ali's legs spread instantly. The cool air crept into her crevice, turning her on even more.

They were moaning, gasping, and breathing heavily. Sarah used her tongue to make a snake like motion from one side of Ali's ribs to the other, then across her stomach, and across her pelvis. Ali felt as though she would spontaneously combust from excitement. Sarah slid down on to the floor, to her knees. The smell of Ali was intoxicating, and her thick, juicy vulva was beckoning for her attention.

"Oh baby, you smell so good," Sarah whispered.

Ali was squirming around in anticipation, which made Sarah's eagerness even stronger. She delved into Ali's sweet smell, with her tongue wildly massaging her clitoris. She went slow and easy, then fast and hard. Sarah stiffened her tongue and pushed it deep inside Ali while rubbing her slick jellybean with her thumb. She could feel Ali's vaginal muscles shuddering over and over.

Sarah pulled her face away from Ali's genitalia and said, "Whew baby, just go with the flow. Don't hold back. I can handle anything your body does."

Then Sarah slid two fingers into Ali's vagina and wiggled them back and forth, as she suckled her clit. Ali felt as though she was losing control of her body. She was screaming, "YES," in her head, and then it flowed out of her like a fire alarm. This ignited a spark in Sarah. She wildly licked, sucked, and continuously fingered Ali, all at once. Ali repositioned her legs so that she could push herself into Sarah's face, and her words became nothing more than guttural groans. Suddenly nothing was coming out of her mouth. Ali felt her stomach doing belly flops. She was feeling indescribable. She only knew it was the best she'd ever felt. The fluids in her body seemed to synchronize, as her body shook and quivered. Joyful tears seeped out of her eyes. Her body released what felt like a gallon of urine. Sarah let out a satisfied moan, and then licked the length of Ali's slit on both sides. This action caused a little more cum to escape, and shivers spread all over Ali's body.

In a cocky tone, Sarah asked, "Oh, are you okay baby?"

Hoarsely, Ali replied, "Oh…My…God! I, I, I…oh wow!"

"I quite enjoyed that too sweetie." Sarah was happy to please Ali.

"Oh my God, did ya feel me cum real big?"

"Mm-hmm and I tasted it too."

"Oh God!" Ali immediately felt embarrassed. "I'm sorry."

"Why?! You have no idea how much that turns me on."

Ali cleared her throat. "It was one of those female ejaculation things wasn't it?"

Playfully, Sarah began to gently rub Ali's inner thighs. "Yes it was baby, and it's all over the bed and under ya. We might need to take a shower." Sarah then stood up and lay down beside Ali on the bed. She kissed her full lips.

"Hey, what is that smell?"

"Uh…that's you." Sarah was matter of fact about that.

Ali gasped. "Oh God! I, uh, do I, is that good or bad?"

Sarah answered, "First of all, every woman is different. We all have different smells and tastes, and honey, there ain't a thing wrong with you. I love your taste, and your smell."

Ali sighed, and then sat up. "Hey! You're bald down there." She expected hair.

"Oh yeah. I like the way it feels."

Nervously, Ali replied, "Oh…did mine bother you, I mean, it's not shaven and…"

Sarah cut her off. "Honey your hair is pretty thin down there anyhow, but I don't mind a little hair. Some lesbians don't like it, but I don't care. Look, ya gotta stop frettin' about every little thing. If I have an issue I'll talk to ya about it."

"Sarah?" Ali's curiosity was getting the better of her.

"Hmm?"

"Can I, you know, touch you?"

Sarah smiled and said, "You already have, right here," and pointed at her heart. Sarah was embarrassed that she'd said that aloud.

Ali lay back on her side, propping her head up on her left elbow. Her eyes scanned over Sarah's naked body, and then she encircled Sarah's nipple with her middle finger. She watched as the areola changed. Tiny little bumps stood up and hardened on it, along with the nipple. "Your nipples are a different color than mine. Are they all different?"

Sarah gazed into Ali's eyes, and reached up to stroke her hair. "Not always. I think it has more to do with ethnicity, sun exposure, and child birth."

"Child birth?" Ali didn't understand.

"Yeah, well it's just somethin' I've noticed. The women I know who have kids tend to have darker nipples. Maybe it has somethin' to do with the milk ducts."

"Hmm." Ali was satisfied with that answer.

"I don't know for sure that's just my own observation."

"Sarah?" Ali had so many questions.

"Yeah?"

"Do all lesbians have toys?"

Sarah laughed. "It's not just lesbians, ya know. Lots of people have toys, whether they're lesbians or straight girls. You don't have any?"

"Well, no." Ali felt as though she was left out of something.

"It's okay if you don't. I do. I have a dick, and a vibrator."

Ali immediately looked at Sarah's muff. "You don't have a dick."

"Yes I do! I bought it; that makes it mine."

Ali laughed. Sarah smiled. Ali looked at Sarah's breasts. "Ya know I never even realized how much I like boobs. I mean they're fun to play with. I even like mine better now. Is that weird?"

"Ali you're not weird. It's just that you're open to what's goin on around ya. It's always been there, but the mystery in it is gone, because your eyes are open to it now. I started to see that sex was just an expression of bein' a human. My opinions on life and the world changed when I started to realize that this is what I wanted my life to be like. It really is like your whole world is changin', and I know that can be scary, but you can do it. Millions of us have done it before you."

"Who was your first Sarah?"

"Well the first guy I was with was Ian. The first woman I was with was Krista. "

"Ian?"

"Yeah, I've been with a couple of men before."

"So how did ya know ya wanted to sleep with a woman?"

Sarah raised her eyebrows. "Well, probly a lot like you. I just had this over-whelmin' urge to kiss her and hold her hand and stuff like that, plus, I always wondered about bein' with a woman anyways."

Ali nodded her head. "I can identify with that." She smiled at Sarah. "I couldn't wait to kiss you."

"I guess I was a little more reluctant than you then. I was scared to touch her even though I wanted to. I think I was afraid I'd like it, and what do ya know? I did." Sarah displayed a huge smile, as she bounced her eyebrows up and down.

"Well how did ya get to the place where ya weren't afraid?"

"Krista made the first move, and I surprised myself by not pushin' her away. I went real slow, as far as touchin' her, and she was ok with that. One day she was standin' over me with her pants down and without thinkin', I just went for it. She said, "Hold on. If you're gonna do that I'm lyin' down." My heart started beatin' like crazy and I knew I had to follow through at that point so I took my time performin' cunnilingus, until I got in the groove of what she liked. After that she told me I was so good that she didn't believe I'd never done it before so I felt good about my skills. That was really when I thought I might be a lesbian, because I wanted to do it all the time, and I kept thinkin' of new things to do with my tongue. It felt more natural to me than lettin' a guy stick his dick in me."

"So…cunnilingus is oral sex?"

"Yeah, it's referring to somebody goin' down on a woman. Felatio is for a man." Sarah was proud to help Ali understand things.

"Well…did you…go straight to oral sex or, I mean, did you use your hand first?" Ali was still questioning her own abilities.

"Yeah. I got really good with my hands first, which is actually kind of a good thing."

"Why?"

"Well if you know what it feels like with your hand first, then you kinda know what to expect with your tongue. Cause you know where the spots are already and how much pressure to use and all that."

Ali bent down and sucked Sarah's nipple, causing Sarah to jump. "So…what does it feel like, in there?"

"In? In the pussy?" Sarah was excited by this line of questioning.

Ali's eyes popped open wide. "I've always thought that was such a dirty word, but…it sounds sexy the way you say it," jested Ali.

Sarah laughed out loud. "Well…it's warm, gushy, soft, and, well you'll find out soon enough baby."

"Yes I will." Ali slowly ran her hand across Sarah's nipples, then down her stomach, and over her vagina. Sarah panted, and then licked her lips. With one finger Ali traced the opening of Sarah's vulva.

Sarah grabbed Ali's arm to stop her. "You'll get in trouble down there honey." Sarah's eyes smiled up at Ali.

Ali's left eyebrow arched higher than the right as she smiled devilishly at Sarah. She slowly pushed her middle finger into Sarah's moist opening, and her legs spread wide. Ali's heart began beating faster. She gulped loudly as she felt the warm stickiness. "You're so hot in there."

"That's what you do to me baby." Sarah's voice was weak.

Ali started moving her finger in and out of Sarah. She could tell she was enjoying it so she pushed harder. Sarah groaned loudly. Ali stopped for fear of hurting her. "I'm sorry! I just wanted to make you feel the same way you made me feel."

Sarah smiled. "Honey, it felt good. I'll let you know if somethin' hurts. Just be careful with those long scary fingernails." Sarah leaned up and pecked Ali on the mouth.

"I can cut 'em right quick!" Ali jumped up.

Sarah reached out for her. "Wait. There's plenty o' time…unless this is a one-time thing."

"One time? But I thought we'd be spendin' a lot of time together."

"Good answer baby, that's what I wanted you to say. It's just that in the past girls like you would lead me to believe there was more goin' on than there actually was. They just used me as a science experiment, ya know, just to be with a woman, but I don't want that with you."

Without thinking Ali answered, "I would never do that to you! I really do like you, a lot." Ali sat back down on the bed, and continued, "I've liked you for a good little while now, but I was scared, ya know, because you're a woman. I even kinda liked you when I was with Justin."

Tears rolled down Sarah's temples and into her ears. She quickly sat up and kissed Ali affectionately. "It's okay babe. It'll all be okay."

They kissed again. Sarah eagerly pushed Ali down on the bed. The look in her eye was as if she were going to devour her. No one had ever looked at Ali like that before; she didn't know what to do, so she just lay back on the bed and enjoyed herself. Sarah licked and slurped inside Ali's labia until she had three more orgasms. Sarah's energy seemed bountiful, as if it would never die, but Ali couldn't hold her legs up any longer. Her body had been so contorted that she had a sore muscle on her rib cage. Finally, Sarah climbed up on the bed beside Ali and snuggled with her. They fell asleep together, with their arms and legs intermingled.

After a few hours, Sarah awoke in bed alone. She called out for Ali but got no answer. She checked the pockets of the jeans she was wearing the night before and found that her car keys were gone. She immediately picked up her cell phone and called Ali, but her voicemail came on. Sarah was nervous. What if Ali had freaked out and decided it was too much for her, to be with a woman? What if she'd gone to work, and told someone about them?

"Oh shit! Work." She called Mr. Stanley, in a panic. She explained that she'd been to the emergency room with a friend until the wee hours of morning and that she was extremely sorry that she was late.

"Sarah, it's okay. I understand. Allison came by and explained how you helped her after her fender bender last night."

"Fender bender?" Sarah was confused.

"That's what she said…that a car hit her from behind and she had to sit at the hospital for a few hours, even though she didn't get hurt. She said you came to her rescue," Mr. Stanley explained.

"Right! Yes sir. She was a bundle 'o nerves. I stayed with her until she relaxed, but listen, it won't happen again, I mean missin' work."

"Oh I'm not worried about that. I believe this is the first day you've missed since I've been here, and I've been here for more than two years now. However, I do need to remind you that fraternization between senior and junior officers is frowned upon, especially when you're in line to be the boss. Look, just get some rest and I'll see you tomorrow."

"Thank you Mr. Stanley. You have a good day."

"You too."

Sarah reminded herself to get her head back in the game. That she couldn't allow herself to be lost in love and mess up her chances of becoming the Branch Manager someday. She'd worked too hard, for too long to get to where she was, and she wasn't going to let anything stand in her way of that dream. Mr. Stanley was set to retire in just three short years, and then she would take over.

Sarah decided to make herself a snack, and then she sat down on the sofa to watch TV. The cool leather felt sexy on her bare skin. She fell back asleep and dreamed of making love to Ali.

Ali opened the front door to hear moans coming from the couch. She snuck over and peered onto the cushions. Sarah was dreaming. She looked so peaceful and innocent. Ali admired her naked beauty, and then heard Sarah say her name. A huge smile appeared on Ali's face. She immediately locked the front door. Her heart was beating heavily; she couldn't wait to touch Sarah and kiss her. She walked to the front of the couch, disrobed, and got down on her knees. She quietly whispered, "I think I could fall in love with you Sarah Ravenal Buckman."

Sarah stirred. Ali hoped she hadn't heard her. She quickly placed her hand on Sarah's left leg, and began caressing her thighs. Sarah's leg slid off the black leather cushions, giving Ali complete access to her moist vagina.

"I'm goin' in, I hope that's okay," Ali announced. She was afraid to touch her without forewarning or permission.

That's when Sarah realized she wasn't just dreaming about Ali touching her. The softness in Ali's voice exposed the sensuality she was feeling. Sarah groggily smiled up at Ali. "I'm all yours baby."

"Your body is amazing Sarah." Ali eagerly kissed Sarah's plump lips, then leaned back to admire her flesh again. "Mmm." She leaned forward again, with her face at Sarah's stomach. In doing so, her foot hit the TV remote on the floor. The channel changed itself to a soft rock station. "Don't Know Much," by Linda Ronstadt and Aaron Neville was playing. Ali smiled at Sarah then bent down and kissed her hard. Lovingly, she ran her hand all over Sarah's body, while sucking on her nipples. Sarah's sounds were turning her on.

Out of nothing more than instinct, she slid a finger inside Sarah. The reaction of sounds that Sarah produced drove Ali's desire to go deeper and faster. She saw that Sarah was at her mercy, which turned her on even more. Ali got the feeling that she was taming the lion that everyone else was afraid of. She watched in amazement as Sarah's body jumped, writhed around, and jerked.

Ali's hand and bicep were getting tired, but she didn't want to stop. "Oh I've gotta change arms baby girl…oh, uh…I didn't mean to call you that."

Sarah's eyes watered as she giggled. She put both hands on Ali's red cheeks. "Why don't you get on top of me in the sixty-nine position? That way I can taste you while you do me sweetie."

Ali liked the way that sounded and quickly straddled her in the opposite direction. Sarah immediately plunged her tongue into Ali's sweet love cave. Ali inserted her other fingers into Sarah. Ali explored the mounds, crevices, and depth of Sarah's vagina. It was incredible; Sarah's pussy was hot and gushy. Her muscles were so strong that Ali thought her hand was stuck a few times. Again Sarah was making her feel so superb that she lost touch with her surroundings, and what she was doing. Twice she reminded herself that her hand was inside Sarah.

She was two inches away from Sarah's pussy. It didn't look or smell as scary as she'd imagined. Ali could hear the sound of her fingers swirling around inside of it. Her curiosity got the best of her. She slid her hand out of Sarah and smelled it. The smell was indescribable, but not nasty or gross. Suddenly she licked her index finger, and surprised herself. It was kind of sweet, and a little salty. Without a thought, she pushed against the arm of the couch with her feet, and pushed her tongue into Sarah. She'd heard to do the alphabet with your tongue, so that's what she did.

Sarah gasped, loudly, and then began licking and sucking Ali harder.

After doing the alphabet several times, Ali knew where the clitoris was, and that Sarah's favorite letters were "O" and "E".

Sarah grabbed Ali's buttocks. She pulled them down so that Ali's vagina was clamped over her whole face.

Ali wanted to feel what was going on inside Sarah now. She slid her hand back inside of her, and flicked Sarah's clit with her tongue.

A long guttural, "Oh", rose up from Sarah's mouth, and vibrated inside of Ali.

This sent chills up Ali's back. She began humping Sarah's face.

Sarah tightened her grip on Ali's buttocks again, then clamped her lips around her clit, and began sucking and licking it simultaneously.

Both ladies were gasping and breathing hard. They sounded like a seventies porno. They pleasured each other until Ali's juices flowed out of her like a waterfall, and Sarah said she couldn't feel her clitoris anymore. Their muscles were exhausted. Ali could barely climb off of Sarah and turn around to snuggle with her.

Sarah smiled, contently. "Wow. If that really was your first time you were born to be a lesbian baby."

"Really? So I was good?" Ali was beaming with pride.

"Mmm. Magical and you'll get even better with time. Mmm, just the thought gives me chills."

Ali snickered. "I didn't hurt you though right? I mean, I know the inside is more delicate than the outside."

"No baby. You were great. You have my permission to wake me up like that any time...hey, where'd you go anyway?"

"Deputy Sparks called so I went to the station. It was either that or he was gonna come over here, and I didn't want him to know that you spent the night."

Sarah stopped rubbing Ali's arm and sat up. "Why does it matter if he knows?"

"I guess it don't really...I just didn't think it was any of his business."

"Are you sure it's not because you're embarrassed?" Sarah's doubts were returning.

"Hell no! You're a beautiful woman and a great person. Why would I be ashamed?"

"That's good to know, but not what I asked."

Ali was confused for a few seconds. "Oh! God no! I'm not embarrassed of us either! I am a little scared though. Not of you, but of me. I mean, who am I now?"

Sarah turned and placed her hand on top of Ali's. "You're still you. Ya just have to accept that your world has opened up a little. Now you have to decide what to do from here."

Ali looked down at the floor. "Well I know my life will never be the same. I can feel it. I mean, everything feels different. Even this mornin', and don't take this the wrong way...but...every woman I saw looked...different. Ya know? It was like I could see beauty in all of 'em. The way they brushed their hair off their shoulders, or the way their nose moved when they talked, or how certain colors made their skin look brighter or more beautiful. I actually looked at boobs and butts. I mean I just noticed so much more than I ever did before. It was kinda weird, but excitin' too. It was like, how could I have never seen this before?"

Sarah replied, "Yeah, your eyes are definitely open now."

"But I still wanna be with you."

"Good, cause I wanna see where it goes. Besides, I use to be where you are. So I do understand. It's like a new beginnin' or chapter in your life. You may even start to realize times that you had a crush on a girl and you just didn't know it at that time. I did. I even had a couple of ladies ask me if I was gay and I'd be grossed out by the idea, well, on the surface I would act like I was, but I wasn't really." Her eyes widened as she continued. "I was intrigued and excited by the thought of it deep down, but I was too afraid to let anybody know. I dated a few men that my mom had picked out. She really wanted to be a grandmother."

"Sarah…I'm not ready to come out. I mean, I just did "it" for the first time. I don't even know if I'm gonna be a lesbian or bi or…go back to men."

Sarah let out a long sigh. "Yeah, I guess it would be selfish of me to wish you'd be a lesbian just so we can be together. And yeah, I guess it does take some time. I didn't come out right away and it was basically okay for me, of course, I didn't realize it at the time. I finally got to the point that I just couldn't stand lyin' to my mom anymore, and I told her. She didn't get mad or upset. She just accepted me."

Ali asked, "How did she do it so easy? My mom wouldn't. I know that for a fact. When I was a kid, my neighbor Mitzy, acted like a boy, and they never let me play with her. I felt sorry for her. She was always alone, until she got into high school. Then she'd always hang around with boys. My dad even called me back up into the yard one day when I was talkin' to her, and we were just talkin' about horses. At the time it just seemed like he didn't like her family or somethin'. Now I know it's because he knew she was gay."

"The older generation is just like that sometimes. That's how they were brought up." Sarah shrugged her shoulders.

"Yeah but she was just a kid. Just bein' herself, ya know?"

Sarah yawned. "Well, that was your dad. How was your mom?"

"She did whatever daddy told her to."

"Well then Ali, you don't really know how she feels about it."

"True…I guess." Ali paused. She thought about the fact that her mother was a counselor. "Ya know I'm sure she's had to deal with gay people at work."

"By the way...it's LGBT; Lesbian, Gay, Bisexual, and Transgender."

"Huh?" Ali was confused.

"Gay women are called lesbians. Some are really sticklers about it because they want to stand out from the men."

"Oh...well I don't even know what that all means exactly." Ali felt self-conscious, and bit her bottom lip as she looked down at the floor.

Sarah was amused, and snickered. "It's ok. I didn't know everything at first either. The most important thing to remember is that the person identifies themselves. You don't know what they are really, unless they tell ya."

"That didn't help me."

"Ok...lesbians: they're homosexual women, but there are subsets within the lesbian spectrum. There are lipstick lesbians, bull dykes, dykes, gold stars, and then people like me who fall between the lipstick lesbian and the dyke."

"Ok, I pretty much know that lipstick lesbians are the girly girls and dykes dress like men, but what is a gold star and a bull dyke?" Ali wanted to make sure she understood.

"Bull dykes are the big ladies that dress in plaid and men's clothes. They don't usually like to be touched, well, occasionally they do. They like to do all the work though mostly."

"By big, do you mean tall or overweight?"

"Could be both, but usually overweight. Their hair is usually short, plain, and styled like a man's. A gold star is a lady who has known her whole life that she was a lesbian, and has never been with a man."

"Wow. That would be weird, never bein' with a guy." Ali couldn't imagine it.

"Or it could be the best thing ever…to know exactly who you are when you're that young and never have to pretend."

Ali nodded her head. "Hmm." That was something to think about. It would be great if people just accepted you for who you are, instead of judging you. People would feel much freer to be themselves. She leaned over and kissed Sarah. "So are there classes of men too?"

"Oh yeah, I don't know all of 'em but I do know about twinks, fairies, and bears."

Ali popped an eyebrow. "What?"

"Twinks are the young gays who aren't very experienced yet. They get to be molded and trained. Now the bears, believe it or not, are the big hairy guys. And yes, I mean tall, or overweight, or both. They're usually short and stocky though. Fairies are the men who act more feminine than a woman, ya know, the flamboyant ones. Then you've got your trannies. They are men who dress as women, like drag queens, but they're not always gay; most of the time they are, but not always. When they're in drag, ya know, dressed like a woman, they want to be called ma'am. Oh, and women don't want to be called sir, usually. Some do, but they'll let you know if they do. Trans-gendered ones have had the surgery already to be in the body they feel comfortable in."

"God! I didn't know there was so much to bein' gay." Ali felt overtaken with doubt.

"It's not about bein' gay Ali; it's about bein' who you are on the inside...human."

"How do ya know who is who?"

"Sometimes ya don't. That's why you just treat everybody with respect, and use pronouns that aren't gender specific. I'll tell ya what...let's go to Atlanta this weekend. I'll take you to Rain Bow Rick's. You'll see everybody there.

"Sounds interesting. But what would I wear?" Ali was excited.

Sarah giggled. "The same thing you'd wear to any club. I'll prob'ly wear shorts and a tank top, depending on the weather, and my kicks."

"Good. I think you'll enjoy yourself, and there we can act like lovers and it will be ok."

Ali looked at Sarah apprehensively.

5

Saturday night finally arrived and Ali was still nervous about going to the club. The weather report said it would be in the seventies that night so she decided to wear a jean mini skirt, a black tank top, and black flip-flops. She wanted to look sexy for Sarah, but also like she belonged there, even though she wasn't sure she would.

Sarah was looking forward to sharing this experience with Ali. Her first time at the club had opened her eyes to the cultures within the culture of the LGBT community and she hoped it would do the same for Ali. She couldn't wait to be able to dance with Ali, and hold her hand, in public. She wondered if Ali realized she could do that there and not be judged.

Sarah's car was only a year old and it was in great shape, and really comfortable. It was a black Buick Enclave, with black alloy rims; she took really good care of it, as there was no trash in it, and it still had the "new car" smell to it. She took so much pride in it because it was the newest car she'd ever owned. Before that she owned a five year old Mini Cooper. She hoped Ali wouldn't mind taking her car since it would look classier than Ali's 2003 Ford Taurus.

Ali's front porch light was on already, and it wasn't even dark yet. She was already thinking about coming home. Sarah hoped that wasn't going to hinder their fun.

She wanted to have a relaxing evening, full of wonderment for Ali. She knocked on the wooden door.

As Ali opened the door, she thought her eyeballs would pop out of her head like a cartoon character. Sarah looked amazing. Her khaki shorts were fitted to her thighs, and the baby blue tank top she had on emphasized the sexiness of her skin. "Oh my God! You look so damn good."

"Why thank you ma'am. You look pretty damn good yourself. Mmm, and your eyes are gorgeous. That blue eyeshadow really makes them stand out." Sarah smiled. "Can I come in?"

"Oh yeah! Come on."

With the door closed, Sarah grabbed Ali's waist and pulled her close. They kissed passionately and caressed each other's backs and breasts. Ali backed Sarah up into the door and slid her hands underneath her shirt. Sarah straightened out her back so that her breasts were pushed out. Ali slid Sarah's bra up to expose her nipples. She began sucking on them, one at a time. Sarah reached out to touch Ali's muffin, but Ali backed the bottom part of her body away.

"Just let me do this, please." Ali wanted to take control.

Sarah looked at Ali intently, and then slowly put the palms of her hands on the door. She was used to taking control, so this was hard for her to just enjoy herself. She usually pleased the lady first then waited for her turn. She decided to just go with it.

Ali slid Sarah's shorts down. That's when she realized that Sarah wasn't wearing panties. Sarah's smell wafted through the air. Ali's instincts kicked in and she straight away got down on her knees, and placed Sarah's left leg over her right shoulder. She kissed Sarah's inner thigh then her left and right labium. "Your pussy is so beautiful. It opens like a tulip. Mmm." The deep sound excited Sarah. Ali dove in to Sarah's lips. She licked all over Sarah's moist cavern, and lapped up its juices. Ali took her time and made sure she licked and kissed every inch of Sarah's soft vagina. She placed three fingers inside Sarah and swiftly moved them back and forth, hitting on her g-spot each time. Sarah writhed around in ecstasy, slightly pulling on Ali's hair. She pivoted, arched, and humped against the door. She felt as though she were going to suck Ali's arm and head up inside her. Finally her stomach stopped fluttering and what seemed like a downpour flooded out of her body, and all over Ali's face. As Sarah arched her back again, to let out all the fluid, Ali licked it fervently, while moaning aloud.

Sarah could feel herself getting weak. "I'm gonna fall," she whispered to Ali.

Ali stood up, picked Sarah up, as if she were carrying her through the threshold, and put her on the couch. Sarah was stunned. She felt so vulnerable with Ali. It was a scary. She would have to gain control back somehow, but at the moment she was too tired.

Ali paused over Sarah, licking her lips. "Mmm. Pineapple."

"Aww baby. Your make-up is smeared everywhere." Sarah saw black eye liner all around Ali's eyes.

"Oh that's ok. Trust me; it was worth it." Ali smiled, licked her lips, and then went into the master bathroom.

Sarah got comfortable on the couch, holding her legs open so she could air-dry. She wanted to fuck Ali with her strap-on. "Hey," she called out.

"Yeah?"

"How do you feel about strap-ons?

Ali stopped washing her face. "Um…I don't know…I guess I kinda thought you wouldn't want to do that to me."

"Why?"

"Cause that's what a man does to woman. Not a woman to a woman."

"Strap-ons are made for a reason. I have one remember? I was just wonderin' how you'd feel about me makin' love to ya with it."

Ali thought it could be fun. "Well why don't ya bring it one day and find out."

Sarah smiled. "Woo-hoo!" The thought of it lifted her spirits and energy. She jumped up off the couch and put her shorts back on, and then headed to the bathroom to clean herself up.

Ali was still in the bathroom putting her face back on. Sarah rounded the doorway and stopped behind her, watching as she carefully drew the eye liner under her eyes. She leaned her pubis against Ali's butt. Ali smiled at her in the mirror. Sarah slowly rolled Ali's mini skirt up. Ali was also going commando.

Playfully, Sarah said, "Hehehe", and then gently pushed Ali over the sink. Once her butt cheeks were spread Sarah bent over and licked Ali's anus, and then began flicking it with her tongue. As she did this she put her right hand between Ali's legs and massaged her clitoris, with her thumb. She used her left hand to caress Ali's nipples.

Ali had never had anyone play with her ass like that before. She was unsure of how to react but she liked it so she just relished it. "Is that a rim job?"

"Yeah baby. Is it ok for me to do that? We never talked about the ass." Sarah lovingly bit the meaty part of Ali's buttocks. She then lightly swatted them. "Is this ok?"

Ali responded. "Uh, yeah. I kinda like that actually."

Sarah smiled. She put her hands on Ali's back and lifted her shirt. She leaned down and licked all around Ali's shoulder blades and bra strap. Then, she put both hands on her covered boobs and softly pinched Ali's nipples. As she did that, she rhythmically humped Ali's naked bottom. Every time she bumped her it pushed Ali's groin into the sink's counter top. The pressure was over-whelming Ali's senses. It felt incredible. She felt like she had lost her inhibitions and screamed, "Oh god! Fuck me!"

Sarah quickly put one hand back between Ali's legs; shoving her fingers into Ali's honey pot, and her thumb just inside Ali's anus. She jerked her hand in and out, and up and down, inside Ali, as quick and as hard as she could. Sarah did this for at least ten minutes before her forearm muscle started to tighten. Ali reached backward and pulled her butt cheeks apart. That let Sarah know she wanted her hand deeper, so she pushed harder and faster. Ali let out a howl. She kept repeating, "Oh yes!" Sarah began humping against her again as she continued filling her holes. Only a few minutes passed before Ali's body weight fell against the sink. Goose pimples rose up all over her back as she ejaculated again. It ran all over Sarah's hand and down Ali's legs. Sarah knew she had control now. It was her turn to pick Ali up, and she sweetly placed her on the bed.

Ali's body quivered all over. "I don't think my nipples will ever go back down. I can still feel you inside me."

Sarah smiled contently. "Good. You remember that tonight when we're around all those other ladies hittin' on ya."

Ali let the remark brush over her. She wasn't thinking about anyone else. "Come snuggle with me."

Sarah climbed over her and lay down. They snuggled until Ali got her strength back, and then they got ready to go to the club.

Melissa Ethridge was in the CD player. Sarah switched it to, "I Will Never Be The Same". "This is my song to you Ali."

"Isn't that a break up song?"

"Well, it can be, but listen to the words. Because of you, I will never be the same."

For the two hours it took to get to the club they talked about work and their favorite music. They both liked rock, classic rock, country, pop, eighties, seventies, and golden oldies. They shared stories about their first loves and why they didn't work out.

Ali's first love was Davey. He was a handsome, sweet, farmhand at the dairy. They were teens when they met. They stayed together for five years. They were about to get married when a friend of his told Ali that he'd been cheating on her. She was devastated. He'd been seeing one of the girls at church. He begged her not to break up with him, saying that he only did it because he realized that Ali would be the last person he ever slept with. That remark burned a hole through Ali's self-confidence. She no longer thought she was worthy to be truly loved. She hadn't spoken to Davey in over a year. She thought about him occasionally. She'd finally forgiven him for cheating on her; citing that she just wasn't exciting enough for him and that she must have held him back from his full potential.

Sarah's first love was Krista. Krista was a voluptuous Chinese-American, with beautiful skin, perfect breasts, and a dynamite personality. She just expected too much out of Sarah, and Sarah didn't know how to be in a relationship, or how to be a step-parent. Sarah was lost on the responsibilities included in taking care of children and she was expected to work her full-time job, take care of Krista's son in the evenings, and do the cooking and cleaning also. Krista went back to college at night, after work. It was too much for Sarah at the time. She often thought about that time in her life and what would have happened if they'd stayed together. She was mature enough to handle all that now, but now was too late anyhow. Krista had decided to go back to men, although she was single. Krista and Sarah stayed in touch over the years. Sarah was very fond of Krista's son, Barrett, and communicated with him from time to time. Krista was important to Sarah, not only because she was her first love, but because she'd learned so much about herself and who she did/did not want to be, from Krista.

The huge parking lot was almost full. They had to park five rows back from the door. As they got out Ali heard techno music. She cocked an eyebrow and looked in Sarah's direction.

"Yeah baby, that's the club."

As they crossed the parking lot Sarah reached out to hold Ali's hand. Ali pulled it away. Sarah said, "You know it's ok to touch me in here. You'll see; it's not like a regular club. Everybody in here is accepting."

Ali was still cautious. What if someone saw them holding hands? They would think they were a couple.

The line to get in wasn't very long. They only had to wait ten minutes. Ali was quiet, taking in all the conversations around her, and thinking of how good it felt when Sarah was fingering her anus. The couple in front of them were making out. She'd never seen two men make out before. She watched them until one of them looked at her. She turned her head quickly. Sarah reached out for her hand again, to remind her that she wasn't alone. This time Ali accepted it.

They made their way up to the counter, showed their ID's, got a stamp on their hands then went around the corner, through the hallway. It was dark. Ali made out the lights to the bathroom doors on the right, at the end of the hall. She clasped Sarah's hand tight as they walked into a huge open room. There were tall tables and chairs, all surrounded by people, talking loudly. She followed Sarah to an empty table in the corner of the room. The dance floor was right in front of them. The music reverberated into Ali's chest. She could feel every beat. Some of the songs she recognized. They were hot hits that had been remixed to add the techno effect.

"You wanna drink?" Sarah asked?

"Uh yeah, how about a Sex on the Beach?"

"Ok." Sarah made her way to the bar.

Ali sat there looking around. She saw men dressed as women, women dressed as men, girly girls, flamboyantly gay men, a couple of bears, and a lot of young men. Most of the men on the dance floor had their shirts off. The girlie girls danced sexy with each other, and there were a few butchy girls that were dancing with girly girls. She scanned the other tables. There were so many people, and they all looked different. She was having trouble making out whether someone was a male or female, even with the way they were dressed.

Sarah finally made it back. "Here ya go."

"Please don't leave me again."

"Ok. Did somebody say somethin' to ya or somethin'?" Sarah was ready to tell somebody off.

"No. I just, well, I'm feelin' uncomfortable."

"Oh…ok. Well, I'm back now. Oh. Guess what? I saw Denise over there."

"Denise? The nurse?!" Ali automatically felt scared that she would be recognized.

"Yeah. Crazy huh?"

"Oh shit! What if she tells somebody she saw us together?"

"Ali! Really? Ok, so what if she did? She'd also have to tell on herself for being here, and she's married, with kids and everything, so I doubt she will."

Ali thought she was probably right. "True."

"Do ya wanna dance?"

Ali ferociously shook her head. "No thank you. I'll watch you though, if you want to. I just wanna sit here and take it all in."

Sarah said, "Ok then." She turned and danced her way over to the dance floor.

She had good rhythm. Ali watched as she broke it down on the dance floor, and then as several women came to dance with her. She recognized Denise as soon as she stepped up to Sarah. Denise leaned over and whispered into Sarah's ear. Sarah smiled. Ali immediately wanted to know what was said. She continued watching as Denise put her hand on Sarah's waist and they danced together. Denise turned so that her backside was facing Sarah, and continued to dance. She placed her hands on Sarah's thighs as their bodies moved in time with each other. Ali wanted them to stop, but she was afraid to go out there and dance with Sarah herself. Denise's hard butt was right in Sarah's groin, and her nipples were hard and pushing through her shirt. She was sexy, for sure. Her slender legs and arms were not as dark as Sarah's but sill tanned. Her hair was pulled back into a low ponytail, and her tiny feet were encompassed by red pumps. They matched her top. Ali anxiously waited for the song to be over. She looked around and noticed an African American male staring at her. She smiled briefly and then turned her head back toward Sarah. A few moments passed.

"Hey." The man who had been staring at her had walked over. He was wearing a flannel shirt that was too big for him, and he was shorter than her. His baggy jeans flowed over his work boots.

"Hey." Ali wasn't sure what to say.

"Is this your first time here?"

Ali could tell now that this was a woman dressed as a man. "Yeah. I'm with my friend Sarah." She pointed at Sarah on the dance floor.

"Cool. I'm with my friend too, Denise."

"Oh? Ya'll are together?"

"Sometimes, well, when her husband is out of town and her kids are at her parents'."

"Oh. Well, Sarah is the first lesbian I've ever known."

The man smiled. "You never get over your first."

"Oh we're not a couple!"

Renee Black

"Right. That's why you wanna shoot Denise right now for touchin' her."

Ali looked down. She couldn't deny that's how she felt. "But…they have a history though."

"History?" The man went straight out onto the dance floor and grabbed Denise by the arm. He was saying something to Denise as she struggled to pull away, but the man was stronger.

Ali could see that Sarah was getting upset and she wished she hadn't said anything.

The man finally walked away and Sarah walked over to Ali. Denise followed.

"That was so not cool. Never tell anyone about somebody else's history. If they want somebody to know they'll tell 'em."

"I'm so sorry." Ali felt horrible.

Denise jumped in on the conversation. "Oh don't worry about her. I was getting tired of her anyway." Denise sat down in one of the empty chairs across from Ali. "I have an idea. Why don't ya'll make a Denise sandwich out of me!?"

Sarah guffawed at the idea. Ali was shocked.

"It is not gonna happen." Sarah was matter of fact.

"You sure do act different here than you do at the hospital." Ali was in disbelief because she said that out loud. She immediately put her hand over her mouth. "Sorry."

Denise stared at Sarah and said, "Oh come on. I know ya like me." Then she looked at Ali. "And you…you have one of the prettiest pussies I've ever seen, and I've seen a lot. By the way, I don't work here. I came here to let loose."

Ali's face was flushed. She didn't know how to respond.

Sarah said, "If you like pussy so much why don't you leave your husband and get a girlfriend?"

"If it was that easy I would." Denise stood up and walked away.

"Are you ok baby?" Sarah was concerned about Ali.

"Yeah. I'm just…uncomfortable."

"Well hang on. The drag show will start in a little bit."

"Really? Drag show? Cool." Ali was still reeling from the Denise issue. "Do ya like her?

"Denise?! No. Not the way I like you. Besides, I have turned her down several times, just tonight. She tried to get me to go back home with her and Deon, to go in the bathroom with her, and then with you and me."

"Oh God!"

"Yeah. I feel sorry for her."

"Why?" Ali was feeling anger toward Denise.

"Well honey, it's obvious that she's unhappy with her husband or she wouldn't be steppin' out on him. I think she's a lesbian that's just too scared to come out because of her family. She's probly worried that they won't accept her, and at this age in life she's too set in her ways and comfortable with bein' a part of society's norm."

"Well when ya put it that way, I guess I feel sorry for her too."

The Divinyls' "I Touch Myself" came on. The whole club seemed to react in unison; everyone started singing along with it and doing their own dirty dancing. Sarah sang the entire song to Ali, while touching her own nipples and crotch area, as she danced. Ali was somewhat embarrassed but couldn't help smiling at her but she seemed to relax a bit.

As the song ended Ali said, "Uh, I hate to say this but I need to pee."

Sarah smirked at Ali. "Why do ya hate to say that? Afraid to walk through the crowd?"

"Well I want ya come with."

"You got it baby." She reached out for Ali's hand.

They walked through the crowd and waited for their turn in the bathroom. As they went in they heard loud breathing. Ali turned and looked at Sarah; her mouth dropped open. She couldn't believe that someone actually had the nerve to have sex in the bathroom. Sarah laughed.

"You wanna give 'em a run for their money?"

Ali was scared. "Hell no!"

Sarah laughed out loud. The noises got quieter. Ali walked on into the empty stall. Sarah followed. Ali turned and looked at her like she had done something wrong. Sarah stepped back outside the stall and held the door closed. When Ali was finished she escorted her back to the table.

For the rest of the night they loved on each other, held hands, watched other couples, watched the drag show, kissed, laughed, talked, and drank.

On the ride home Ali inquired as to whether it was common for straight couples to be at the gay club.

"Believe it or not, the gay community accepts everyone, even straight couples. There were a lot of straight couples there tonight, but if you walk into a straight club you won't find many gay couples. They're too scared to go into a straight club. There's too many bashings, and have you ever heard of a person bein' straight bashed by gay people? No. It don't happen that way."

"Wait. You're gay and you go to the Inn with us."

"Yeah but you never see me take a date now do ya?" Sarah was smarter than that.

"Oh. No. I don't."

"So...how did ya like the Drag Queen and Drag King show?

"The queens are the men and the kings are the women right?"

"Ali, didn't you listen to the announcer? He told you when they changed courses."

"That's what I thought, geesh!"

"Anyhow...how did ya feel about the club, minus Denise and her crap?"

"Well it definitely felt different from the Inn. I didn't feel like I had to watch what I said or did. I just felt free to be me. If I had wanted to take my shirt off I think it would have been ok."

"Ali! You can't take your clothes off at any bar! But I get what you're sayin'. It is more uncluttered because it has no societal demands. In the LGBT community you're not expected to be one way or the other, you're just accepted for who you are. Well...except if you're bi. Sometimes the community frowns on that 'cause they don't understand how you can like both. That's mostly the older folks though."

"Hmm. Well I learned a lot, and I did have fun. I'm pretty sure I saw a group of "trannies," and are threesomes big in the lesbian community? I mean were we suppose' to sleep with her?" Ali was still confused about what she was expected to do.

"Don't you get it? You do what you want to do, not what somebody else expects out of ya. If ya wanna have a threesome then have one, but nobody expects you to. That's the difference between the LGBT community and the heterosexual community. We look at a person's humanity, not their sexuality."

That made sense to Ali. Why judge somebody else? Why did they feel like they had that right? Her world did seem like it had lots of rules. If you're a girl you marry a boy and have kids. If your husband wants to invite someone else into the bedroom with you, you're supposed to do what he wants. Mothers are supposed to take care of the kids. Fathers are supposed to do the yard work and take out the trash. Females are supposed to make less money than men and do as their told. "Well there are a lot of rules."

"Yeah but wouldn't ya rather just be yourself, and do what you wanna do; what makes you happy?"

Ali thought about that, and how that life would be. Could she handle it? Would her friends accept her that way? Would her family treat her the same, or different? Would they still talk to her? Would she really be happier? She was already happier with her love life, but would that flow over into her regular day to day life?

6

The past few weeks had flown by. Ali was seeing beauty in all the females around her, but especially in Sarah. It was hard to work with her every day and not be able to touch her or speak to her very much. Ali would catch herself staring at Sarah, and then abruptly turn her head. One of the other tellers had seen her do this several times.

"So…Ali…is there somethin' you need to tell me?"

Erica Smalley was the short, petite, darkly tanned teller that she worked with. She looked at Erica and said, "What are you talkin' about?" She couldn't afford for anyone at work to find out about her and Sarah since either or both of them could get fired. Also, she didn't know what the other girls would say about her.

"Well, I mean the way you keep lookin' at Sarah. You got a crush or somethin'?"

"What?! No! That's weird."

"Hmm, me thinks she doth protest too much." Erica's left eyebrow jumped up higher than her right, and then she crinkled up her nose.

At that moment a car pulled up to Erica's window. Erica turned her attention to the customer.

"Thank God, saved by the car," thought Ali. Luckily, the lines stayed busy for the rest of the day, and she didn't have to talk to Erica anymore.

Ali knew that she loved Sarah, more deeply than anyone else she'd ever been with. Her biggest fear was that her friends would not want to be around her anymore, if they found out that she liked both men and women. She wasn't looking forward to telling her mom about it either. Although every time she talked to her mom she wanted to tell her that she'd found an honest, real love. She was beaming inside, when nobody was looking, except Sarah. Ali finally felt alive, like she truly knew where she belonged, and why she'd been unhappy for so long. Her life seemed to be turning around, at every turn. Her rent and insurance premiums had gone down, Georgia's summer season had begun, work was going great, and to top it off, she had Sarah's love and attention. Life was going good, all except for not being truthful with her friends and family, about who she really was. Her conscience was getting the best of her. She knew she'd have to say something soon. She felt as though she was denying her love for Sarah by not speaking up, and that love was too pure and uninhibited to squander away.

Later that night, Ali asked, "Sarah, how did you come out?"

"Oh, so you do think about it?"

"Of course I do! I wanna tell everybody about us. I'm just kinda scared."

"Well Ali, there's lots of horror stories about comin' out. My story is different than most though, I guess. My mom is old school about datin', but she just kinda knew, even before me. See, she still believes in the Native American ways of my grandfather. In that culture there are homosexuals, but they're called "Two-Spirit or Berdache." It's usually men, but over the last few years they have seen that a woman can also be a Two-Spirit."

"So…in your culture it's ok to be gay? I mean, really?" Ali was intrigued.

"They don't look on 'em with disappointment or judgment. They're revered for having two points of view to share with the rest of the tribe, as in male with female tendencies and vice-versa."

"Cool for you." Ali felt like that didn't help her at all.

"See, actually, she thought I was a Two-Spirit, even when I was a kid, so when I came out to her, it was no shock. However, I have friends who were kicked out of their house for bein' gay, and then I also have a few whose parents have just accepted 'em, and a couple who still act like their partner is just their best friend. It all kinda depends on your parents and how strong you are. That's a bell you can't unwring, ya know, so you have to be ready for all the stuff that comes with it. That's why I said it also depends on how strong YOU are."

"Well, I don't wanna make anybody uncomfortable." Ali liked being liked by everyone. She saw that as her social standing.

Sarah politely answered. "Well honey, there comes a time when ya gotta stop worryin' so much about what others think and make your own happiness."

"Make my own happiness? But I need help. I mean, I need information on how to do it, ya know?"

"I'll tell ya what…let's watch a few movies and shows, and then if you still need more help I'll let ya talk to my friends."

They watched all seasons of *The L Word*, and *Queer as Folk*. They continued by watching *The Real L Word*, *Grey Matters*, *The Incredibly True Story of Two Girls in Love*, and *Go Fish*. After two weeks of being inspired by what she saw, Ali felt as though she had a deeper understanding of the whole LGBT community, and herself. She identified most with Max, from *Go Fish*, and Jenny, at the beginning of *L Word*; probably because they were going through such an eye-opening changes in their lives. She realized that for others to accept her she first had to accept herself, and she wasn't sure yet if she could.

"Well, now that you've watched all this what are ya thinkin'?"

Ali shrugged her shoulders. "I'm still scared. I mean, what if I'm only gay with you?"

"What?" Sarah chuckled. "Honey, you look at other women don't ya? See somethin' special about other women?"

"Yeah but I only want to touch you, kiss you, be with you."

"That's because you're in love with me. If I wasn't in the picture you'd be with some other lady. I'm sure of it."

Ali wasn't so sure. "But I only had the nerve to sleep with you because of the rape. I mean, what if that had never happened? Would I still have made a move on you?"

Sarah got a chill. Where was this going? What was Ali thinking? "Ali, I think it was goin' in that direction anyhow, maybe the rape sped it along, but, yeah, I think we would have ended up sleeping together eventually. Don't ya feel like it was meant to happen?"

"I do, and it has changed me, but, for the better?"

"You wanna crawl back in the closet now? I see it's too hard to be out, huh?" Sarah was disappointed. She thought they were making progress.

"Sarah, I'm bein' serious. I don't know what to think or do now."

"Baby, ya gotta be yourself."

"I don't know who I am though. I mean, I know I love bein' with you and talkin' with you, but what about men? Am I just never gonna get to sleep with a man again? What about them?"

"What about us Ali?"

Ali didn't want to lose Sarah. "Well I still want to be with you, but I can't tell anybody. I mean, it's just not that easy to "come out" for everybody else, like it was for you."

Sarah was quiet. She thought Ali was getting ready to break up with her, so she prepared to act tough; like it didn't bother her. She didn't want to make Ali feel uncomfortable either, but she knew it would be better if she'd "come out." Then, they could just be together, without all the lies that they had to tell Ali's friends and family. "Ali...if you need me to go so you can figure out what you want just say the word."

"I don't want you to go though." Ali felt desperation set in. Her eyes teared up.

"Ali, I can't stay if you're not gonna be real with me, cause you're not givin' your all, and I am. I refuse to let myself be treated this way again. That's what Marie did to me."

"What? What did she do?" Ali was curious.

"She got me all twisted. I fell in love with her the first time we went out, but I didn't know how to be in a long-distance relationship the second time. Every time I saw her she was high. I felt like I was puttin' in my all, and she was so selfish. She was just in a different place in her life. We both were and it didn't work out at all. The sex was great but the rest of it got in the way and by the time we broke up I had hurt my family by choosing her over them, sold a car I loved so that I could go see her every weekend, and didn't know why it happened. I was suicidal because I was unsure of myself. Which way should I go from there? She went back to men and I felt like it was my fault. I flip-flopped between men and women searching for something and it took a while for me to realize that I just couldn't be with HER; love just wasn't enough. I never wanna feel that way again. I felt so defeated, and like a loser. I wanted it to be like it was the first time, at the beginnin' of our relationship. I had held out hope, for too long, that we could re-ignite our passion. It just didn't happen. The reality set in and I was a mess. I was very depressed, and I stayed away from everybody. I felt like it was my failure, but it was hers too, but I felt it, she didn't; she was high."

"So she escaped into her pot?"

"Basically." Sarah nodded.

Ali was beginning to understand why Sarah was so worried about being hurt. "So she was into men the whole time, but sleepin' with you, makin' you think she wanted you?"

"Yep. That's it in a nutshell, and she was escapin' because she was afraid to "come out" again. She worried about what her co-workers would think about her, instead of how she truly felt."

"So…are you sayin' you can't be with me if I don't "come out"?

"Ali, I want to be with you, whole-heartedly, but you're not puttin' your all in. I know there is more that we could do together, like go out in public, for one. We could go to my mom's house, your mom's house, out to dinner, to a movie, ya know, things that normal couples do. All we do is make love, watch TV, and stay home. I love spendin' time with you ok, so don't get me wrong, but I want more, I deserve more."

Ali was angry. "I…can't, give you, more, right now!"

"I'm sorry Ali, but it's just not good enough anymore. It's been two months and you don't wanna meet my friends or my mother. We never go anywhere together. We stay locked up in YOUR house, cause you won't come to mine. I honestly feel like…like you're embarrassed by me, but I know now you're actually embarrassed of yourself." Sarah stood up and slid her crocs on. She turned around to face Ali, as she sat on the bed. "We need… no, YOU need some time alone, to think. Call me when you make some decisions." Sarah walked out of Ali's house, calmly closing the door behind her.

Ali cried for three solid hours. She went through a surplus of emotions, from sorrow to neediness, then to anger. She shouldn't be forced to "come out" if she wasn't ready. Sarah was being unreasonable. She wished Sarah was there to hold her and comfort her. She was going to take this chance to have a night alone and maybe even a week. She'd see if Sarah made her gay, or if she already was and Sarah was just the catalyst for letting it out.

Sarah was a mess. She was so emotional over leaving Ali that she thought about going back and just letting her do whatever she wanted. She really missed Ali. She'd devoted every waking moment to pleasing Ali, and treating her like a goddess. She couldn't do it anymore though. It was time to think of herself also. She deserved the same unbridled passion that she'd been giving to Ali, and how could she get that from somebody who was afraid to love her? It would be too easy to allow Ali to stay in her life, hidden away, because at least she'd be there, but it wasn't enough.

Sarah drove to Lou's house. It was a cute little mother-in-law's cottage, behind a huge Victorian style home. She shared the driveway with the owners of the big house. Her job was to take care of the animals on the land. Lou was a fifty-three year old bull dyke. Lou and Sarah had become friends when Lou needed a loan from the bank. A friendship developed instantly. She appeared to be the strong silent type, but she was actually a teddy bear inside. Her looks were definitely deceiving. She had graying blonde hair, huge breasts, she was slightly overweight, and had big green eyes. Her favorite shirts were flannel, and she always wore work boots.

Sarah knocked on the door, and got no reply. Lou's car was there though, so Sarah looked around outside and saw her in the pen with the goats. She walked over to her. The bucket in her hand was almost empty.

"Hey lady." Lou's gruff voice greeted Sarah.

"Hey, can I talk to ya?"

"Sure. I'm almost done." Lou walked over to the gate and let herself out. "I've gotta get one more bucket full then I'm all yours."

"Ok." Sarah patiently waited for her friend to finish feeding the goats. She looked around the property at the wide open field, at the beautiful green grass, and at the mule in the distance. She squatted down and petted one of the kids. A nanny ran up and butted her on the backside. Sarah fell over, face first. "Shit!"

Lou laughed loudly. "You ok girl?" She was trying to hold it together.

"Damn it. Yeah, I'm fine." Sarah dusted off her face, arms, and clothing. "That's pretty much how I feel; like I've had dirt thrown in my face."

"Well damn! What's up?" Lou's concern came through.

"I just had a stupid fight with Ali and I walked out on her."

"What did ya do to her?"

"Lou, why do ya always assume it was me?"

"Well Sarah, because it usually is."

Sarah sighed. "Well this time I was standin' up for myself. I told her I couldn't be with her if she wasn't gonna put her whole self into the relationship."

"So…basically you told her she had to "come out" or y'all couldn't be together." Lou always had a way of making Sarah see what her actions looked like from the outside.

"Yeah I guess." Sarah was beginning to see that she'd said the wrong thing.

Lou looked at Sarah. They walked over to Lou's cottage and sat on the back porch. Lou lit a Winston one-hundred. "Well…number one, ya gotta take care of yourself, so I understand your point of view. Number two however, you can't expect her to "come out" if she isn't ready. No matter how much you love somebody else you always gotta love yourself more. She's scared about her family not acceptin' her, but she's prob'ly more scared about acceptin' herself. If you're truly the first woman she's been with then she don't know any better yet, ya know? Her whole world just started changin', and you're a part of it so I wouldn't be surprised if she wasn't bein' passive aggressive with ya. She ain't meanin' to but I bet she is."

"Well kinda. I mean, she was kinda short with me, but not until I told her I wanted more."

"Oh, you gave her the "I want more" speech. So now she's also thinkin' she's not enough for ya anymore."

"What! But that's not what I meant. It would be great with us if she was just willin' to "come out" so we could do more together. I feel like a kid with a brand new awesome toy, but I can't tell any of my friends or family because it might get taken away."

"Well y'all could have come over here, anytime."

"Yeah but that's the point; she won't go any place with me. She's afraid to be seen with me, anywhere."

"Well she went with ya to the club."

"Yeah, she did, but that's two hours away. She freaked when we saw Denise."

Lou giggled. "Is that little spitfire still chasin' ya?"

Sarah smirked and rolled her eyes, with a slight nod.

"So how'd ya leave it with Ali?"

"Well, I told her to call me when she's made some decisions."

"Sarah…you have basically told her she can't talk to ya if she's not willin' to "come out" which means you're not gonna be there to help her along. You've isolated her to make some of the biggest decisions of her life, alone."

"Oh shit. I didn't mean to." Sarah propped her elbows on her knees and put her face in her hands.

"The problem is if you go back on your word now she's gonna think she can just stay in the closet and you'll just go through life as her dirty little secret."

"You're right. I guess I'll have to stick with it, or accept what I don't like."

"Well don't give up on her yet. Just give her some time alone. She'll do what she feels is right. It may not be what you want, but I know you love her enough to want what's best for her."

Sarah paused. "Yeah I do. I just want her to be happy." Lou gently nodded her head in agreement. "Well thanks for bein' my soundin' board. I'm gonna go grab a salad from Zaxby's. I'm starvin' like Marvin. You want anything?"

"No but thanks. Hey, I'm here if ya need to come back and talk."

They hugged and Sarah left. On the way home she was listening to the radio and "Dirty Little Secret", by All American Rejects came on. She cried. She didn't want to be Ali's dirty little secret. She wanted to be her friend, lover, hero, and protector. She hoped against hope that Ali would see she wasn't trying to be mean, that she just wanted what was best for both of them.

The next few days were so lonely. Sarah couldn't get the thought of Ali out of her head. Memories of her touch, her smile, her smell, her orgasm faces, and her sweet voice kept coming back to Sarah. She wondered if Ali was thinking the same things about her.

7

Work was excruciatingly depressing. Ali was continually fighting urges to look at Sarah, and talk to her. She was still angry that Sarah had given her an ultimatum and at work she acted hard and cold, so that Sarah would think she was unaffected by their distance, but at night, she'd cry herself to sleep and imagine Sarah was there holding her. She'd dream that they were lying naked together, snuggling, and making love. Sarah's smell and touch were still so fresh in her mind. She yearned to touch her, and felt a physical sickness because she couldn't.

"Ali!?" A familiar voice resonated in her head. It was Justin. He was standing in front of the counter. His dark brown hair was almost hidden by his John Deere baseball cap. His black jeans and Wolverine work boots looked brand new. Apparently he was doing alright financially. His familiar smile brought a smile to Ali's face.

"What are you doing here," asked Ali? Her face turned red and she immediately looked to see if Sarah was watching. She wasn't.

"I wanted to see ya."

"Why? We haven't talked for like eight months." Ali's tone was spiteful.

"Ali, why are you actin like that? Can't I just stop in and say hey?" Justin was hurt. He'd hoped she would be happy to see him.

She glanced over his shoulder to see if Sarah was looking. She was. Ali smiled and in a flirty tone said, "Oh you know me. I'm just emotional. So what are you up to these days?"

Justin smiled back at her. "Yes I do, and I ain't up to much. I dated a girl for a month, but we broke up last week. It was nothin' special."

"Yeah…I was with somebody for a while too, but we're, um, on a break, I think."

"Well good. You can join me for dinner."

Ali looked again to see that Sarah was watching. This will make her jealous, thought Ali, with a coy smile. "Well sure. Why not?"

Sarah couldn't believe that Ali was trying to make her jealous by flirting with a guy. She was so stubborn. Ali was going to make herself miserable before she came around. Sarah wondered how long that would take. Ali was being immature. Sarah called her friend Lou, to complain. Lou reminded her to be patient and if it's meant to be it will be; that Ali had to "come out" on her own terms.

Justin and Ali went out several times. Ali still missed Sarah though. Justin was boring but safe. She imagined everyone would be boring, compared to Sarah. On the third date they went to see *Mockingjay Part One*, in the theatre. She noticed some sexiness about Jennifer Lawrence that she'd never seen before. J-Law had blossomed into an attractive young woman. She got turned on.

"She's really hot," whispered Ali. Justin agreed with her.

They went out to dinner afterwards. Justin was rubbing her leg under the table. Then he looked at her breasts, through her shirt. She saw him and it flattered her; she wasn't sure she wanted to have sex with him but she'd have to because that's what society expects. "I saw that." She was distant in her words.

"You're still sexy." Justin complimented her with a grin.

"Thank you." Ali wasn't giving him any signals.

Justin's grin left his face. "You're still thinkin' about the other guy aren't ya?"

Ali paused and looked at him intently. She wanted to say, "You mean woman," but she knew that wouldn't go over well. She looked down at her spaghetti. Her appetite was gone. Why had Mr. Loverboy turned her into this? Why did he ever open her up to her own desires? This could be so much easier if she was just with Justin, like before. She felt she wasn't being fair to Justin. "I'm sorry."

"He must have been one hell of a guy if he's got ya all twisted up like this." He re-positioned his baseball cap, and then turned to look out the window, at his Ford Ranger.

"I don't know what to say Justin." Ali was quiet.

A few minutes passed and then Justin turned his face back toward Ali. "Well, let me try to make you forget him." He leaned over and kissed her hard.

His kiss was slobbery and sloppy. She remembered him having good kisses. What had happened? She wanted Sarah's sweet, juicy, sexy kisses, and that made her kiss him harder. She had to get over Sarah's influence on her. "Let's go back to my place," she offered.

"Hell yeah!" Justin was all for it.

"I'm gonna go take a quick shower ok?" Ali was intent on proving that she could be with someone other than Sarah, and that she wasn't gay.

"Ok. I'll be waitin' for ya."

Sarah would have taken a shower with her. She wondered why Justin didn't offer to. She quickly shaved her legs and underarms. She thoroughly washed her muffin so it would be fresh when he went down on her.

Justin was lying on the bed naked when she walked out of the bathroom. His farmer's tan was the first thing she noticed. Then she realized how hairy he was. The hair wasn't attractive to her. In fact it was repulsive. She made herself walk to the bed. She was determined to sleep with him; she had to, to prove she could.

"Oo-wee! Come here girl." Justin was excited by Ali's flesh.

She sat down on the bed and waited for him to make the first move. He reached his arm out and ran his hand down her arm. Ali thought it was sweet. Then he immediately put his hand between her legs. His rough hands were coarse on her skin. "Easy," she scolded.

"Sorry."

Justin slid his middle finger into her vagina. She slid her legs open. He kissed her neck. Shivers went down to her nipples. She lay back on the bed. He bent over her and kissed her as passionately as he could. She reciprocated somewhat. He then lay beside her like Sarah used to. He fondled her left breast, and then kissed her neck again. Her nipples stiffened. She could feel his penis rubbing against her leg. It felt cold. Had it always felt cold? She sat up and looked at his manhood. It was still the same. It didn't look any different. It was still a circumcised six inch penis. There were no crevices or caverns on it to explore. It was like a rubber bone hanging off of his pelvis. She wasn't sure what she wanted to do with it. She cupped it in her hand and squeezed it gently, then pulled on it a little.

"Yeah baby. Put it in your mouth." Justin wanted her to taste him.

She positioned herself over his groin area. She licked the head of his dick, and then slowly sucked on it. Justin pushed her head down hard, making her gag. She decided she'd had enough of oral sex with him. She placed her hands on either side of his shaft, and rubbed it up and down. She looked at his face. He was laid back with his eyes closed, not even looking at her. His medium sized hand enclosed his penis shaft and he jerked it about.

"This is what I want." His words seemed callous.

He abruptly stopped rubbing himself and tumbled Ali over onto her back. She gasped in surprise. He shoved his middle digit back between her vaginal lips, and jaggedly pushed it in and out. She grimaced from the clumsy thrusting of his hand. She wished he would perform oral sex on her. Maybe that would be good. She couldn't even remember if he was any good at it. Suddenly he leaned down and pulled her legs far apart, and then pushed them into the air. He stuck his mouth between her legs and blew into her hole. She put her legs down.

"What are ya doin?" Ali was disappointed already.

"Sorry. I can do better."

Justin stuck his tongue out as far as he could and used just the tip to flick her clit. He started moaning. His tongue was just wet and icy. He seemed to be just rhythmically licking, in the same spot, over and over. She felt she could do a better job herself. She moaned as if she were enjoying it; she didn't want to hurt his feelings. She couldn't wait for him to put his cock inside her. There was no way he could screw that up.

"Fuck me Justin." She was ready to try something else.

He eagerly slid his penis into her vagina. He pumped it in and out, then swirled it in a circle. His strokes were short and fast. Ali was enjoying it a little, but only when he was swirling around inside her. She opened up her legs as far as she could. She wanted more. He didn't go deeper though.

"Harder." She thought a verbal cue would help him.

He pounded so hard against her that she could hear his testicles slap against her bottom. He did this for a few minutes. She still wasn't getting the feeling she wanted. He arched his back and she knew that meant he was ready to blow so she groaned as if she were too. What a waste of time. She was less than appeased. He shook and breathed hard, and then rolled off of her. She looked at him and wished he was Sarah lying beside her. This didn't work out the way she thought it would, and she knew for certain he wasn't Mr. Loverboy. She wanted to snuggle but he got up and went to the bathroom. She turned on the stereo with the remote. Katy Perry's, "Thinking of You" was playing. How fitting, she thought. She couldn't get Sarah off her mind, and she wished she were there instead of Justin.

"It's a good thing you haven't changed the house around. I still know where ya keep the towels and rags."

"Yeah they're the same."

"And so are you. You haven't changed a bit. Well, except you didn't do that thing with your tongue. I've really missed that."

She honestly didn't miss it after all. In fact, she didn't miss anything about being with a man. What she missed was being with her woman Sarah, and her house may not have changed but she sure had. Or maybe she was always this way and just didn't realize it. "Hmm." She gave him a one word response because she didn't care to converse with him anymore.

He sensed that she was bored. "Ya ready for me to go?"

Admittedly, and with hesitation Ali answered, "Yeah."

Justin seemed to get his feelings hurt. He quickly dressed and left, without saying good-bye.

Ali showered again. She lay down on the bed and listened to her ipod. She played "Satisfaction", by the Rolling Stones, several times. She thought to herself that the only satisfaction she would get would be from Sarah or Mr. Loverboy. She fell asleep with the ear buds in her ears.

The sheets were being pulled off of her body. Ali looked up and saw her rapist. This time there was no dress or bra in the way. She'd laid down nude. Her hands were not tied above her head. Mr. Loverboy gently ran his fingers across her bare skin again, exciting her nipples and vagina. As he straddled her and bent down to take her nipple in his mouth, Ali reached up to grab his back. She needed an actual connection. He softly pushed her arms away. Every time she tried to touch him he pushed her arms and hands away. His touch was effeminate. He stroked, caressed, sucked, licked her body, and made love to her like Sarah use to. Ali began to cry, thinking of Sarah.

Her sniffle got his attention. Mr. Loverboy brought his face up to hers. His mask was pulled up above his mouth. She could smell herself on him. Hoarsely he said, "What's the matter with you? Did I hurt you?"

She was shocked to hear a soft spoken whisper. "Uh…no, you didn't. You just make me miss somebody."

He immediately got off of her and stormed out the door.

Ali was flabbergasted. That was two men in the same night that had stopped before she was able to orgasm. What was wrong with her? She wanted Sarah in the worst possible way, and sat up to call her.

The phone rang and rang, but Sarah didn't answer. Ali left a message. "Hey Sarah. It's me. I'm sorry I haven't talked to you in a while, but I miss you. The rapist was here again and I need somebody to talk to. I'm hopin' that can be you, but if not I'll understand. I'm home, awake, and I'm probly not goin' back to sleep so…call if you want to. Okay, well, I lo…uh, talk to ya later." She almost said, "I love you!" What the hell was that about? She was so confused.

Ali went to the living room to watch TV. She watched a marathon of Law & Order: SVU, until she fell back asleep. She dreamed that Mariska Hargitay was lying beside her on the couch. She and Mariska, aka Olivia Benson, were making out and pawing at each other's bodies over top of their clothing. In the dream, Ali couldn't stop telling Olivia how sexy she was.

Sarah listened to the message that Ali left. She felt compassionate about being Ali's friend, even if they couldn't be lovers, because she still cared about her well-being. She drove to Ali's house. The whole way there she told herself that they couldn't touch, because it would be detrimental to what she needed in her life. Sure the sex was fantastic, but she still wanted more; physical and emotional.

Justin's truck wasn't in the driveway so she went and knocked at the front door.

The door opened slowly, revealing more and more of Ali's naked body.

"Oh shit!" Sarah was embarrassed for Ali.

"Sarah? Am I dreaming?" Ali was half asleep and wiping her eyes.

"No, now let me in before the neighbors see you naked."

"Naked!" She looked down. "Oh shit! Get in here."

Sarah was pleased to see Ali's beautiful curves. A smirk spread across Sarah's face, as she followed Ali into the bedroom and watched her put on her red silky robe. "You probly shouldn't answer the door when you're half asleep Ali. You might forget you're naked." Sarah giggled.

"Well, its nothin' you've never seen before." Ali was quite turned on by being in the buff around Sarah. She licked her lips in a sexual manner, and then sat down on the bed, exposing her vagina.

Sarah's heartbeat sped up, her chest heaved, and her eyes darted up and down; between Ali's face and her vagina. She licked her lips. "You're so not playin' fair. I…I gotta go." Sarah turned toward the front door.

Ali jumped up off the bed and wrapped her arms around Sarah, and held on tight. "Please!" She could smell her own vagina; she was so excited to be near Sarah.

Sarah didn't want her to let go, but she needed her to. "Okay, I'll stay but let go of me."

Ali removed her arms from Sarah, very slowly, while running her palms across Sarah's breasts.

Sarah's eyes closed and she sucked in her top lip. She didn't want to say what she needed to say. Faintly, she said, "You don't get to do that anymore." She looked up at the ceiling then turned to face Ali. A single tear was traveling down her right cheek. Sarah sighed. "Ali…I didn't mean to make you cry okay? It's just that I need more, and yes, I do want it with you, but not now, not until you're ready to really put yourself in my life, because I want all of you, not just the part that no one knows about. I want your crazy looks, your sweet smile, your fun spirit, your cute laugh, your bodacious body, your wonderful brain, your kind heart, your innocence, your naivety, and your…I just want it ALL! Okay?"

Ali cried harder. Both cheeks were moist with tears, and her face was red. She was unsure of what to say, but she blurted out the first thing that came to her mind. "Well if we want each other then why aren't we together?"

"What don't you get Ali?! I said I want ALL of you, not just what little you're willing to share. I need all of you. I deserve all, of my partner. Yes, I hope that can be you, but it's not gonna be right now, cause you're too afraid to be yourself."

"But Sarah, I want you. I know I do."

"Oh yeah? Then why are you goin' back out with Justin? Just to make me jealous? Well, it's not workin', and I'll tell you why. It makes me think you're immature and not ready for a real relationship, especially if you can just bounce back and forth between us. How do I know that you really do want me?"

"Sarah…I just do. Nobody gets me like you do, not Justin, not anybody. I don't even like havin' sex with him. It…"

"Sex?! You had sex with him already?! God damn you!" Sarah briskly walked out the front door.

Ali called after her but she didn't even turn around. Sarah was really mad. Five minutes went by and Ali received a text message from Sarah. "*If what we had was so special then y did u sleep with him? Obviously I mean nothin 2 u.*" Ali cried for an hour. She didn't reply because she didn't know what to say.

Sarah was beside herself in depression. She thought Ali would have come around by then, and not slept with anyone else. She hadn't. She called her friend Sam. Sam had been her best friend since the seventh grade. They could talk about anything and everything. Sam was a party girl at heart but her heart was always in the right place. She was accused of being Sarah's lover as a teen, just because they hung out together so much, but that was untrue. Sarah looked at her like a sister, and knew that Sam would be there for her no matter what. Sam was always optimistic about Sarah and her capabilities. She would be there to build her up when she felt down, and celebrate with her when life was good. Sam was the first friend that Sarah admitted to being gay to. Sarah suspected her immediate acceptance sprang from the fact that she'd overcome her own diversities. Sam was an albino, who was legally blind, from a broken family, but had still managed to come up in the world. She got away from her family as soon as she was sixteen. Sam got her GED and then put herself through college. She'd moved to several different states as an adult, and explored. Sarah respected her opinion and advice. Sam was her oldest and dearest friend. She was working as a hotel manager in California. With her golden blonde hair she fit in right away.

Sarah explained to Sam what had happened.

"Absence makes the heart grow fonder Sarah. Give her some time. Either she'll realize what she's missin' or she'll stay in the closet. Either way you deserve better than what she gave you. Maybe she's not the one. I know you think she is and I'm sorry to just come out with that but…"

"No, Sam. She's the one for me. I've been in love with her since before we even slept together. I just wish she wasn't so scared to "come out" to her family and friends. We'd be fine if she did."

"Now Sarah you know how hard it is to "come out". Maybe it was easy for you but it's not like that for most people. Remember Patty? Her brothers stopped talking to her, and her parents disowned her."

"Yeah…ok…you're right."

"Of course I am…I'm the great and powerful Sammie." She chuckled.

Sarah giggled. "Thanks for listenin' and settin' me straight."

"Straight? No, no, no. It's gayly forward. You taught me that."

"Thanks girl." Sarah smiled to herself. She decided to give Ali some distance again. Maybe this time she'd realize what Sarah had been trying to tell her, and get up the courage to "come out".

"Love ya Sarah. Gotta go. Carrie Underwood just arrived."

"Sweet! Ooh, get me an autograph. Talk to ya later."

8

It was a typical Wednesday morning. The bank was quiet. It wouldn't speed up until almost lunchtime, when it was supposed to close. Ali and Sarah were playing their normal staring game with each other. Neither of them had gone to the Golden Ridge Inn over the past few Tuesday nights, for fear of running into each other. Sarah was finding it ridiculously hard to stand her ground and not call Ali. Ali constantly thought about Sarah, and the time they spent together. She wanted to keep Sarah in her life but was just afraid of who she was becoming with her.

Suddenly, the front door swung open and a man wearing a mask ran in. Ali flashed back to the rape. She jumped down behind the counter. Sarah saw her and stood up from her desk and quickly came to the door of her office. All the employees gasped, some screamed, but all of them reacted. Sarah sprang backwards into her office and hurriedly pressed the emergency button. She peered back around her office door at the masked man. He was waving a handgun around, as if he wasn't sure what to do next.

"What do you want?" Sarah was nervous but thought she could speed up this process if she cooperated fully.

He turned the gun on her and held it steady. "I want everyone out of their offices and out here now!" His tone was commanding.

Mr. Stanley came around the corner from the vault room, with his hands in the air. "Everybody do as he says."

Sarah and Mr. Stanley slowly walked toward the counter. Sarah leaned up on her tip toes to look at Ali. Ali was on her knees, peaking at Sarah through her fingers. The faint sound of a siren was in the distance.

"I want all the money. Now!" He threw two duffel bags at Sarah.

Immediately she plopped them on the top of the counter and yelled for Ali and Erica to empty out their drawers. The siren was getting closer. They threw the bundles of money that they had in the bags.

"Come on!" He was agitated.

As soon as both girls finished Sarah threw the bags at him. He tried to catch them and dropped the gun. Sarah rushed at him. She punched him in the stomach and kicked him in the leg, but he got the gun before she could. He snatched her around by her hair and pushed the barrel of the gun into the flesh of her arm. She stopped moving.

Ali yelled, "No!"

The police cars pulled into the parking lot. "Damn it!" The masked man pointed the gun at Ali. "You get these bags. We're takin' your car."

"We don't need her. I can carry the bags," Sarah speedily interjected.

Without a second thought, Ali grabbed her keys and ran around the counter. "My car is out the back."

The man pushed Sarah down by her hair. "Get the bags."

She lifted them and he dragged her toward Ali. He aimed the gun at Ali and pointed toward the door. The three of them swiftly ran out the back. There was one cop outside the door. He yelled to the man to freeze. The masked man turned and shot the cop, and he fell over, clutching his stomach. Both girls began to see that they were in deep trouble.

"You drive," he ordered. Ali was terrified but got right in her car and cranked it up.

He pushed Sarah into the back seat and made her slide over, and then he sat down, pointing the gun at her side. "Go bitch, and you better lose the cops or your girlfriend gets it!"

Ali couldn't believe it. How did he know about them? She couldn't deal with it right now. She was too worried that he would shoot her or Sarah. She cautiously drove through town and then to the outskirts. "Where do you want me to go?" She looked up at him through the rearview mirror. He answered with directions to an old abandoned warehouse.

Sarah sat quietly, drinking in her surroundings. She guessed that the man was white, about six feet tall, and around two-hundred pounds. She reminded herself of those details over and over. She wanted to give his description when they made it out alive, if, they made it out alive.

The warehouse was abandoned as usual. Sometimes teenagers would populate the parking lot, but apparently not on Wednesday morning at ten. Ali parked the car and turned it off.

"Ok ladies, no funny business, and nobody gets hurt." The man seemed calmer all of a sudden. "I just want to do my thang and get out of here." Ali thought his voice sounded familiar.

The three of them got out. Sarah noticed a tiny whirlwind of dirt further out in the lot. A whirlwind represented chaos to her, and that's exactly what she was experiencing at the moment. She could feel her feet slipping around in the good old Georgia red clay. She slipped down to the ground, landing on her side. The man helped her back up. He took the bags from her as they entered the rusty old tin building. It was sweltering hot inside. There were a few pallets left over from when it used to be a feed and seed store. Ali and Sarah both stared at each other, as if they needed to make sure the other was alright. They still hadn't spoken a word to each other. He made Sarah handcuff her right arm to a metal pole, and then he made Ali cuff her left arm to the same pole. They both sat down on a pallet. He walked to the back of the building, through the shadowy room.

"Are you ok?" Sarah broke the silence.

"Sarah you shouldn't have run at him."

"I got scared, ok?!" Sweat was running down Sarah's neck.

"I freeze when I get scared."

Sarah nervously smirked. "Yeah, I know." Sarah thought of how Ali put the freeze on their relationship.

The water stopped running and the man walked back toward the ladies. His mask was off. Ali closed her eyes so she couldn't see his face. He laughed.

"You already saw me."

Ali opened her eyes. It was her ex-boyfriend. "Davey?" She was shocked.

"You know him," Sarah asked?

"Yeah…it's Davey."

"It's too hot to keep that damn mask on." Davey wiped the sweat from his face. "You're lookin good Ali."

Ali gulped. "Are you gonna kill us too?"

"No baby. Not unless ya'll cause a ruckus." Davey smiled.

Sarah cleared her throat. "What ARE ya gonna do with us? Wait a minute, Davey? As in…your first love?"

Davey squatted down in front of Sarah. "Why ya wanna know? So you can knock me over again?" His face looked angry. He directed his attention to Ali. "So…I was your first love huh?"

Sarah didn't know whether to be angry, sad, or scared. "I didn't know what to do, ok? I thought you might hurt Ali and I just reacted."

Ali's head jerked in Sarah's direction. Sweetly she asked, "You did that for me?"

Sarah gently nodded her head and whispered, "Yeah". She was just beginning to realize the risk that she took to protect Ali.

Davey sat Indian style by Ali's legs. "Ok…what the hell is goin' on here? Are ya'll like together or somethin'?"

"No", Sarah answered.

Ali looked at her in disbelief. "We should be, but…"

Davey's phone rang. He got up and walked back to the rear of the building.

Ali and Sarah were staring at him. They could hear that he was angry. He was saying, "No, that's not quick enough. I need you here now." He hung up the phone, and yelled, "Damn it!" They stole a quick look at each other while he walked back toward them.

He squatted again, this time in front of Ali. "Looks like we're gonna be here all night, so you girls get comfy." His anger toward them had returned.

"All night? What about Casper?" Ali closed her mouth quickly, and looked down.

"The fuckin' cat will be fine. Ya need to be worried about your damn self."

"Listen Davey, we won't tell anybody it was you. You can just take the car and leave." Sarah thought if she talked to him directly his anger would dissipate.

"You dike bitch. Shut the hell up. I don't know you like that."

Sarah looked at Ali. "Tell him."

"What?" Ali was perplexed. She wiped the sweat off her brows.

"Ok, what the hell is goin' on with ya'll?" Davey was agitated with their closeness. He looked back and forth at them.

"We won't tell anybody, I swear it." Ali was sincere. She noticed how Sarah's chest was glistening with sweat at the rim of her off-white silky tank top that accompanied her suit, and couldn't help but look at her breasts.

Davey saw Ali looking at Sarah with longing. His eyes squinted as he was in disbelief. Could they be sleeping together? Well, of course, why else would she have jumped on him? She wanted to keep Ali safe. The dikey bitch is in love. He smirked. "So is she any good at goin' down on ya?"

Ali gasped. "What! You don't have to dignify that with an answer Sarah."

A rush of confidence swam over Sarah. "She's the best I've ever had!"

"And she's the best I've ever had." She proudly smiled at Sarah.

"Oh shit! I didn't think ya already done it! Damn it!"

Ali and Sarah looked at each other with a wanting desire.

"Fuck. Ya'll are makin' me sick." He reached out and backhanded Sarah across the face. Ali reached out to stop him but he caught her arm. He took her hand and placed it on his crotch, making her squeeze his penis. "This. This is what ya want. Are ya missin' it? I'll give it to ya."

"No", yelled Ali! "You're disgustin'." Ali was surprised at how little she cared about offending him.

"Please, just leave her alone." Sarah spoke for Ali.

"You shut the hell up!" Davey was exuding anger, all over Sarah.

Sarah smiled. "You're just mad 'cause she said I'm better than you." She sat up and pulled her suit top off as much as she could. The rest of it lay in a wrinkled mess on her right wrist; against her half of the handcuff. Tears rolled down Sarah's swollen cheek.

Davey reached out and hit her again, this time in the mouth. She laid her head down on her shoulder.

"Stop it! You can fuck me." Ali wanted him to stop hurting Sarah.

"No Ali!" Sarah didn't want Ali to give up her dignity.

Davey laughed out loud. "I know I can! Ya didn't have to tell me that." A serious look spread across his face.

Sarah and Ali were both in tears now. They looked at each other. Both of them were willing to compromise their respectability and sanity for the other.

Davey pulled Ali's legs apart. He unbuttoned her capris. "Watch how a man does it bitch."

"Please don't." Sarah was begging him not to hurt Ali.

Davey laughed out loud again. He pulled on Ali's legs until she was in a laying position. He unzipped his pants and then pulled Ali's bottoms down to her ankles. Ali looked away from him and at Sarah. As he entered her Ali jumped. Sarah hastily grabbed Ali's hand. A few seconds is all Sarah could stand and she kicked Davey in the knee. He punched her in the nose. Ali cried harder. Sarah slumped over backwards. When Sarah became conscious again Davey put his hand on Ali's neck.

"Do that shit again and I'll choke her." He continued raping Ali.

Sarah held on to Ali's hand for the rest of the time he was inside of her. They looked at each other, trying to fade out what was happening. Sarah mouthed, "I love you" to Ali, several times.

When Davey was done he got up and zipped back up. He left Ali laying half naked and crying on the floor. Sarah lay next to her and wrapped her arms around Ali's waist. They snuggled until they fell asleep together.

"Wake up!" Davey was getting ready to leave. It was daylight again. He walked over to them. "Whatever." He bent down, placing the handcuff key on the pallet, behind Sarah. "I'll be back if ya tell who it was. I'll kill ya both. Oh, and ya better wait to leave until I'm gone." He walked over to the door and dropped Ali's car keys. The sound of a large truck cranked up, and then pulled off after a car door slammed.

"Baby are you ok?" Sarah was in tears again. She touched Ali's shoulder.

"Yeah, but I need help getting' my clothes back up." Ali seemed like a lost little girl.

Sarah pulled up one side of Ali's clothing as she pulled up the other. Once she was dressed properly and sitting up she asked about the key.

"He put it right here. Didn't ya see him do it?" Sarah was concerned that Ali was in shock.

"Huh? Oh. Ok."

Sarah unlocked the cuffs from their wrists, then stood, and helped Ali stand. She walked over to the front door and inspected the parking lot. Ali's car was the only one there. She walked Ali out to the car, holding on to her arm. She loaded her into the passenger side. Sarah got into the driver seat and drove back to town. They didn't say a word to each other. They had to pass by the bank in order to get to Ali's house. There was a cop car in the lot.

"Well, there's a cop. I guess they're still looking for us. I'm gonna turn around and let 'em know we're ok."

Ali pleaded with Sarah. "Please don't."

"We have to Ali. Everybody will be relieved we're ok. Then we can tell 'em to go get Davey."

"What? No! You heard him. He'll come back for us. I don't want him to come back."

"Ali…we have to. It's the right thing to do."

Ali knew she was right. "Ok, but I want you to do all the talkin'."

"Ok. That's fine baby."

"Ms. Buckman! Are ya ok? Where's Ms. Carter?" Sparks saw Sarah as soon as she exited the vehicle.

"Yeah. We're ok. Look it was Davey Reese, Ali's ex-boyfriend. He raped her and smacked me around a little."

"I see the blood and swelling." He reached out to touch her face.

"He left in a big truck. It sounded like a Ford F-350 or somethin' big like that. He only left about twenty minutes ago. I don't know which direction they went, but he had us at the old building on 80 that used to be Buck's Feed and Seed."

"Ok. I'm gonna call it in. Mrs. Carter is inside waiting for Allison. She was here all night."

"Alright I'll tell Ali." She walked back to the car.

"Ali your mom is in here. She's real worried about ya."

"I can't look at her right now. She can't see me like this. I don't know what to say."

"Ali…get out of the car. Now. She's your mom. Just talk to her. Be honest. Maybe she can help ya."

Ali looked at Sarah with disdain. "You didn't get raped. You don't know how it feels." A slow steady stream of tears inched down her cheeks.

Sarah crouched down by the open car door. "Look, I know how ya feel. I was raped when I was twelve. It sucks. But I can tell ya from experience that ya have to talk about it for it to go away. It's gonna take time. It won't happen overnight, but ya will feel better. I'm here for ya, and I'm sure your mom will be too."

Ali looked down at Sarah. Her nose and lip had dried blood on them. Her right cheek was swollen. "Oh God. I can't believe he did that to ya." She placed her hand on the side of Sarah's neck. "I'm so sorry."

Sarah placed her hand on top of Ali's, and then pulled it in front of her mouth, and gently kissed it. "Baby, you have nothin' to be sorry for. None of this was your fault."

Ali looked back down at Sarah. "You have to believe that was not the Davey that I knew. I, I have no idea what happened to him." Ali felt as guilty as if she'd robbed the place herself. Had he picked up on some small detail that helped him to rob the bank? Did he pick that bank especially?

"Ali!"

Sarah stood up and turned around. A pleasantly plump middle-aged woman was jogging toward the car. The lady had the same facial features as Ali. Her eyes were wildly passionate and her light brown hair was beginning to gray at the roots. Sarah stepped aside. She assumed that the lady was Ali's mom.

Ali burst into tears and began wiping them away. Mrs. Carter brushed past Sarah and stuck her arms in the open car door. She pressed herself in and squeezed her daughter. Ali seemed to melt into her. It was obvious they loved each other very much. Sarah couldn't help but wish Ali would let her be the one she melted into.

"Come on Pumpkin; let's get ya to the hospital." Mrs. Carter was taking control of the situation. Ali got out of the car, glanced at Sarah, hugged her, and then went with her mother.

Sarah suddenly felt alone. She crossed the parking lot and watched as Ali and her mom drove off, and then she entered the building.

There were ten cops walking around inside. Some of them had evidence bags. They were collecting anything they thought could help. Sarah walked around them and into her office and closed the door behind her. She plopped down in the chair, let out a sigh of relief, and cried. She wanted to yell but didn't want to draw attention to herself. Guilt weighed heavily on her. She wondered if the events would have unfolded differently if she hadn't rushed at Davey and hit him. She also wondered how Ali would cope with a real rape, after being spoiled by Mr. Loverboy.

A knock came at the door. Sarah hastily wiped her tears away and cleared her throat. "Yeah?"

"It's me. David Sparks."

"Yeah, come on in."

Sparks entered and sat down in a seat across from her. "Ms. Buckman, how are you dealin' with this?"

"I'm ok; I'm just worried about Ali." More tears ran down her cheeks.

"Well she's with her mom. You can go to the hospital after you talk to me."

Sarah broke down. She couldn't hold in her culpability any longer. She told him how she'd pressed the emergency button and ran at Davey.

"Why exactly DID you do that?" He was trying hard to understand everyone's behavior. "Is it because you're in love with her?"

Sarah looked down at the floor. "He pointed the gun in her direction and I was afraid he'd kill her. I don't know what came over me honestly. I just reacted."

"Most people freeze around guns Ms. Buckman. They don't run at 'em." His friend had been shot. He needed to know why. "Did you know Davey was gonna rob the place?"

Sarah quickly looked up at him. "I did not. I'd never even met him before yesterday." She could feel herself growing angry.

"Do you think Ms. Carter knew about it?"

"Hell no! She was surprised when he took his mask off."

"Well it's some coincidence that it just happened to be her ex-boyfriend, then isn't it?"

"Yeah, it is." She was to the point that she wanted to yell. Tears of anger welled up in her eyes. She stood up from behind her desk. "You've got the wrong idea Mister, and I'm ready for you to get the hell out of my face."

Sparks sneered. He'd gotten under her skin, but why? Was she hiding something or were they really innocent? "Ok, but don't leave town. I'll have more questions."

"And I'll have the same damn answers." Going to jail was not on the top of her bucket list. She reassured herself that as long as she told the truth they would be fine.

9

"Tell me what happened, please. Maybe I could help," she begged. Betty Carter couldn't stand seeing her daughter so sad and depressed. "Come on Ali. I just wanna help."

Ali sat quietly, looking out the window. The hospital looked as uninviting as ever. She didn't want to get out of the car. She just wanted to smoke a cigarette, take a shower, and get in bed. Ali knew her mother well enough to know that if she didn't get out soon that she'd have a nurse come out and get her. She didn't savor the idea of going through all the procedures again, but knew she had to.

"Come on baby, there's so much out in the world today we need to make sure you're ok. There's no tellin' what you came into contact with. You may have a small scrape that could turn into sepsis. Let's at least have them check you out…did he hurt you? Did he hit you? Did he do worse than that?" Betty's mind was all over the place. She hoped Ali would tell her what happened.

In a cold tone Ali replied. "Davey robbed the bank mom. He took me and Sarah hostage. He raped me and beat her, and then this morning he let us go."

Tears gushed out of Betty's eyes. "Oh my God! I'm so sorry." She leaned across the seat and hugged her daughter. "There are no words that can make you feel better right now, but just know that I'm here for ya, I love you, and I'm so glad that you're still alive."

A lonely tear trailed down Ali's face. "Let's get this over with." She opened the door, got out, and then walked into the hospital.

Finally her name was called. She was in the waiting room for two hours. Denise called her to the door. She turned to her mom and asked her to stay there. "I need to do this on my own."

Denise quietly said, "No mention of the club in here."

Ali nodded and followed her into a room. It looked just like the other one; boring. Denise acted very professional, yet endearing at the same time. She asked the same questions and ran the same tests as before. As she examined Ali, she hummed. Ali was anxious and wanted to get it over with.

"Can you do it faster this time?"

"I only extract the sample. I have to wait on the lab in order to get the tests back, so it depends on how busy they are as to when I'll get 'em. Just...relax as much as possible. I'm sorry this keeps happenin' to ya."

"Thanks, I guess." Denise was so nice at the hospital. What a contrast to her behavior at the club. "I want you to know that I know you asked Sarah to sleep with you, and what ya did to her before."

Denise peered at Ali over her knee. "Well she was my first. It was exciting and different."

"Yeah but you can't play with people's hearts like that." Sarah deserved better.

"Are you out?"

Ali sighed. "No."

"Well then...isn't that the pot calling the kettle black?"

"Yeah I guess it is." Ali lay her head down and longed for time to pass quickly. Sarah deserved better than her. She was damaged goods now for sure. She remembered the look on Sarah's face while Davey was raping her. It was sheer horror, yet love. She didn't think she would have made it without Sarah. Sarah kept her grounded in sanity, through the whole ordeal.

The test results came back negative. She was thankful. The first rape didn't seem like rape at all, not compared to this one. This time it felt real. It wasn't like a fantasy or good experience. Sparks was right about one thing though; sometimes it's the people who know you that rape you.

Ali took a leave of absence from work. She stayed at her mom's house a lot. She and her mom had many discussions about the robbery and rape. She received text messages and phone calls from Sarah, at least every other day, but didn't return any of them. She wanted Sarah to move on, but with her, but she was afraid to come out, and be touched. She worried that "Mr. Loverboy" would come back to her house and have his way with her, but what she worried about more was that she wanted him to. Her mom told her that most people don't want to have sex for a while after a brutal rape, and that was true for her, but she missed Sarah. Sex was different with her. It was sensual and meaningful. She knew for a fact that she never wanted anything to do with Davey again. He must have been on drugs. If she was gonna be with a man it would be someone like "Mr. Loverboy"; someone who was patient and sensual, like Sarah.

Ali spent a lot of time with her brother, Rob. She wondered if he could ever do such a thing to a female, as rape her. He tried to make her laugh about lots of things, but she didn't. She would just mope around watching TV and smoking. Betty had enough of Ali's moping and one day she called her on it.

"So? This is who you are now?"

Ali looked at Betty. "What?"

"Come on baby. You can do better than this."

"Mom it's only been a couple of weeks."

"Yeah. That much of your life has passed by and you're still stuck here, not living. You should be out with friends. Go see a movie. Get your nails done. For God sakes at least take a shower." Betty was frustrated.

Ali looked down at her clothes. "Do I stink?"

"Well Rob smells better than you these days and he drives a trash truck."

"Yeah? There is somebody that I've been thinkin' about."

"Well go see him."

"It's Sarah mom. She was there ya know? She understands what I've been through. I have been thinkin' about callin' her."

"Sarah? But she rushed him and pissed him off."

"No. She saved me. She was there for me when nobody else was."

Betty didn't know what to say. "Well honey do whatever you want to, you're goin' to anyway."

Ali went home and took a shower. She was looking forward to seeing Sarah. She decided to go back to work.

Monday morning couldn't come fast enough. When Ali entered the bank everyone smiled at her. She snuck a look into Sarah's office. She wasn't there. Ali looked around and found her in the bank vault room. She settled in after a few of the girls welcomed her back. She watched as Sarah crossed the floor staring at her, and banged into her doorframe. Ali giggled and then looked around to see who else saw it. No one seemed to.

Ali's phone vibrated. She looked at it. It was a text message from Sarah. It read, *"Hello beautiful, welcome back."*

Ali looked at Sarah and smiled. She replied, *"Thnx 4 evrythng u have done 4 me & 4 callin & textin all the time."*

Sarah answered, *"Y does it sound like ur sayin bye 2 me?"*

Ali looked at Sarah. She texted, *"U need 2 move on im damaged goods now."* She hoped that Sarah could just be happy, even if it meant that they couldn't be together. The love that they shared would live on in her heart forever.

"No ur not. Ur lovely, wonderful, strong, sexy, smart & a survivor."

Ali cried when she read Sarah's text. She quickly walked to the bathroom. Sarah followed her, and wrapped her arms around her. Ali cried into Sarah's shoulder.

"Is that what you want me to "come out" to? Bein' subjected to rape?" She peered up at Sarah.

"No baby. I never wanted that to happen to ya."

"Yeah, well it did, because I slept with you!"

"No, that happened because of a bigamist, close-minded, jackass. Not all guys are like that."

Ali turned and walked out the door. Why did she say that? She wanted to get closer to Sarah, not farther away, but if it meant she would be subject to rape every time a guy found out she was interested in women, it wasn't going to work. For the rest of the week they had no communication.

"Sparks."

"Yes sir?"

"That small swab of DNA finally came back. It belongs to a female."

Sparks couldn't believe his ears. Maybe he heard it wrong. The precinct was pretty loud. "Did you say female?"

Captain John Dukes nodded his head.

"So a female's DNA was found along with Ms. Carter's at the scene of the rape?"

The Captain sighed and then said, "Yes".

They looked at one another questioningly.

"Let me see that," Sparks said, as he took the paper out of the Captain's hand. He read aloud. "It is the finding of this lab that the DNA in question is XX, which indicates that it belongs to a female. We have searched the database for a match but have come up empty. We can offer insight into the genetic make-up, but only with a 40% accuracy, as the specimen was very small and could have been cross-contaminated with the victim's DNA. Therefore, it is our belief that the said specimen belongs to a non-traditional Caucasian American. It points toward a Pacific Islander, Native American, or Asian ancestry." Sparks sat down hard in his chair. A look of dismay rested on his face. "So…it was a chick…a chick rapist? What the Hell!"

"It looks that way David…unless…"

"What John? What?"

"Unless, she's sleepin' with a lady." John put his hands up and shrugged his shoulders.

Sparks looked down at the floor, shaking his head. It was definitely possible that she was sleeping with Ms. Buckman, but wasn't it also possible that Ms. Buckman had been "Mr. Loverboy"? He took out his notes. Small hands for a guy…not very tall for a guy…gentle…sensual…a mask, because obviously Ms. Carter knew the assailant…hazel green eyes, well Ms. Buckman had brown eyes, but there is always contact lenses…as for the appendage, well women use strap-ons every day, why not? Sparks had a lot to think about.

"Honey?"

"Ma'am?"

"How is work goin'?" Betty was still concerned about her daughter.

"Eh. Alright I guess."

"That's all you have to say? You've been back for a week."

"Well mom, honestly, I stare at the door when I don't have anybody in line. I'm scared he's gonna come back through the door and take me again."

Betty put her arms around Ali's neck. "Baby, I really think you should go to counselin'. I'm afraid you might be goin' through PTSD."

"Ugh! Again? I just don't wanna?"

"Ali...you would rather feel like this all the time? I mean, you know it could really help you. It might even help you to start hangin' out with your friends again."

Hmm. Ali wondered if it could help her to repair her relationship with Sarah. "Alright, alright. I'll go."

10

Ali caught herself daydreaming that Sarah would come out of her office, walk behind the counter, pick her up, and carry her home and make love to her. Sarah's words and her mom's words replayed in her mind. Did she really need counseling? Then again, maybe an objective point of view could be beneficial. She called and sat up an appointment on her lunch break.

A week had passed. Sarah noticed Ali didn't come back after lunch. She inquired as to her where-abouts. Mr. Stanley told her that Ali had a doctor's appointment. Sarah was disappointed that she would have to wait until the next day to see her.

The gray concrete steps looked cold and uninviting. Ali was still hesitant about going to the mental health clinic, but if it could get her mom off her back it was worth it. What's the worst that could happen? The orange brick building was reasonably new; only about ten years old. It was on a small street in town, across from the Department of Family and Children Services, and only a block from the library. The building itself was almost an "L" shape. It appeared that it was two wings. In the front there were long ramps going up either side; that were also gray concrete. The lot shared parking spots with the Community Center for older citizens; it was half way full. She parked right in front of the first office window on the left side of the building. Ali looked around to see if there was anyone there that she recognized. Then she decided that if there was she could just say she visiting her mother. She had five minutes until she was supposed to be inside. She finished her cigarette and threw it on the ground. She sighed and slowly got out of her car, forcing herself to walk up the ramp to the front door.

As she stepped inside a few older people said "afternoon". She smiled politely and said, "Hello". She signed in and sat down. The waiting room was small. A long fold out table sat in the middle of the room, surrounded by six chairs. Chairs also aligned the walls. There were only four people in the room. She didn't recognize anyone. "Wednesday's must be slow, all over town," she thought. There were vending machines in the corner, and she was craving a Pepsi so she bought one. She looked through the glass of the office. Her mother passed by and saw her. The look on her face was that of surprise. She stopped in her tracks, stepped backwards and smiled at Ali, as she waved. Ali half-heartedly smiled back. "Oh great, she saw me. Now what is she gonna do" thought Ali? Betty disappeared from her sight. The door to the left of the office opened and Betty called Ali into the hall.

"What are ya doin here Pumpkin?"

"I have an appointment with somebody named Deanna Hall."

Betty was elated. "Good. She's around your age and she is great at what she does. She has been here a little over a year and she can definitely help you."

Ali was aggravated already. "Great…look I don't want any preferential treatment because of you. I, kinda wanna do this on my own, ok?"

"Oh, ok, well you just go back out there and wait." Betty turned around and walked into the office.

Ali went back through the door to the waiting room and sat down. She didn't mean to hurt her mom's feelings but she felt as though this needed to be done on her own terms, without any extra help, just like everybody else. She wanted to do it right, that way she could find the benefit in it. She waited for thirty minutes until she was finally called.

"Carter." The door opened to a petite lady, who appeared younger than Ali. She was about 5'3 but with her heels made it to Ali's height at 5'6. Her fingernails were in pristine condition, as if she'd just had a French manicure done. Her open-toed shoes revealed red toenails; also newly done. She had big brown eyes and shoulder length, straight, blonde hair. Her nose came out to a rounded point, but it wasn't too long. It fit her face perfectly. She was appealing to the eye. Ali followed her down the long hallway. She noticed that Deanna's flowing shirt clung to her sides, and her slacks clung to her hips. Her skin tone was that of the average Caucasian.

"Here we are. Have a seat." Deanna pointed toward the red leather chair across from her desk.

"Thank you," Ali answered timidly.

"So we have a lot of stuff to go through. Everything is electronic now so there's less paper involved. Have you ever had counselin' before?" She sat down as she asked.

"No. My mom works here so…how's that gonna work?" Ali wanted to make sure her words would be confidential.

"I thought Ms. Betty might be your mom. The resemblance is unmistakable." Deanna crossed her hands over her stomach and sat back in her office chair. "Well, for starters, anything you say to me is confidential. I won't tell your mom anything unless you ask me to, and even then I need written permission. If you were under eighteen it would be a different story."

Ali was relieved. "Thank God!"

"Yeah…so basically today we are gonna get your mental health and medical history. Then you have to see the doctor and the nurse before I can schedule you for counseling." She sat up on the edge of her chair and started typing on her computer.

Ali agreed with a nod of the head. "What do you need to know?"

"Let's start with poly-substance."

"Huh?" Ali wasn't sure what that meant.

"Drugs and alcohol."

"Oh. Well when I was younger I used to drink a good bit and smoke pot sometimes." Ali thought these questions were gonna be easy.

"Ok. So alcohol was your first choice?"

Ali thought for a moment. "Well, yeah, I guess it was. I mean, I drank more than I smoked. It was just certain people that I smoked with, but I would buy the Wild Turkey and drink alone."

"OK and when was this?"

"From about 2003 to 2005."

"And what made you stop Ms. Carter?" Deanna always liked to know what the cause was for stopping.

"Oh. Well, I didn't have the money for it anymore, but also, I saw that it was in the way of my job. I got fired from Wal-Mart for attendance, and that was what kept me out mostly; was the hang-overs and feelin' sick."

"Alright. What about harming yourself? Have you ever attempted suicide or cut yourself or anything like that?"

Ali looked down at the floor. "Well…when I was a kid I would nick myself or scratch my skin off with pencil erasers."

"Ouch. A blade would have been faster." Deanna's voice turned to empathy. "Did you feel better afterwards?"

"Yeah. I would get a rush of happiness. My parents thought I was just a klutz. My mom really got on to me one time though when she saw that I had erased my initials into my leg. I think I was about fourteen at the time."

"Do you still do that?"

"No…now I just mess up all my relationships." Ali smiled. She was feeling more at ease.

Deanna smiled. "Lots of people do that; you're not alone."

"What about hallucinations? Do you hear or see anything that others don't?"

Ali looked away from her and back at the floor. A teardrop fell from her eye. "I see spirits and sometimes I hear 'em."

"How long has that been going on?"

"Since I was four. I told momma about Uncle Billy comin' to see me one night, and how he kissed me on the forehead and said good bye. She slapped me and told me to quit lyin', so I have never really told anybody about it. She had just found out that he was dead."

"You said "spirits". Is that what you believe they are?"

"Yeah. I've seen 'em since I was a kid."

"How do they make you feel?"

"Well the shadow people are scary, but usually I see 'em just as they were, so I'm not scared. If I do get scared I just close my eyes and pray."

"You said your mom slapped you. Was that common? Have you been through other kinds of abuse?"

"Momma didn't like spankin' me or my brother. Usually, she would tell daddy and he'd spank us when he got home. She was verbally abusive though, when I was younger. Now we get along pretty good, and she treats me better. She was depressed a lot. Since she's been on anti-depressants she has gotten so much better."

"Well did your dad spank you a lot?"

"Not really. He would spank me though, even when it wasn't my fault. I got in trouble a lot because of my brother."

Deanna detected a hint of jealously. "Did you feel that your brother was treated better?"

"Definitely. He was a momma's boy and still is."

"What about sexual assault?"

"My uncle molested me when I was three until about seven. Momma didn't believe me on that either. Now this."

"Hmm." Deanna didn't know all this about Betty and would never have suspected it.

"My ex-boyfriend, and first love, robbed the bank where I work, and took me and Sarah hostage. He raped me and smacked on her."

"Oh my God! Is that why you're here now?"

"Yeah." To Ali it sounded worse than it actually was. "If Sarah hadn't been there it would have been worse.

She held me and told me…wait. Do you swear that what I tell you is confidential?"

"Yes of course."

"She told me she loved me."

"Is she your lover?"

"Not right now, but I hope she will be again. I think I'm in love with her but how can I be? She's a lady and so am I. I have never been attracted to a woman before her. It's just her. I mean…I find lots of women attractive, like you for instance; you're really cute. But she is just so…so…I don't know…everything."

"Ok. I'm going recommend counseling for you. I can counsel you or there are two other ladies, well one, because you can't see your mom, even if you wanted to."

"I feel comfortable with you."

"Ok. Good. After you see the doctor and the nurse we can begin. Again, anything you say to me stays with me."

"Thank you Deanna. I need all the help I can get." She went on to answer questions about her family's mental health and physical health.

She walked out of the office feeling ten pounds lighter. Saying it all out loud made it so real and made her feel weak. She held a lot inside. It was time for it to come out. She spent the rest of the evening thinking about how her life would be different now that she would be divulging everything about herself. It wasn't as scary as she thought it would be. She imagined it would help.

A month had gone by. Ali and Sarah still hadn't spoken, except to say hello. Ali had already begun counseling and taking an anti-depressant. She was feeling better emotionally, and having fewer nightmares about Davey. She'd learned that her reaction to the rape was normal; some women want to have sex more and some want no sex. She had realized that her recent experience with Justin was just her way of reaching out for a true, honest connection that wasn't tainted by fear or force. Also, she was looking down on herself for not seeing that Davey was capable of being so violent. She was questioning her ability to choose the right people to surround herself with.

On her third encounter with Deanna she talked about Sarah. "She's just everything I want. She's beautiful, inside and out."

"I'm really not seeing the problem between you two." Deanna was trying to make Ali think about what she'd said.

"She's a female though." Ali couldn't get over that.

"Ok. So? Are you attracted to her?"

"Yes I am."

"Do you want to sleep with her, touch her, and kiss her?"

Ali's nose crinkled up. Now she was being asked the hardest question of all. It is one thing to admit an attraction, but quite another to admit to wanting to sleep with a person of the same sex. Hesitantly, she said, "Well…"

"I'm not going to pass judgment on you. I just want you to really think this through. This decision can dictate your future happiness, and I want you to explore all sides of it." Deanna cared for Ali as a human being and wanted her to see the truth. She gently rocked back and forth in her office chair.

"Truthfully? I…yes I want to wrap my arms around her and hold her forever. I'm scared though."

"Ali, are you scared because of the vulnerability of being in love or are you scared you're gonna go to Hell?" Deanna had been through this before with other patients.

"Well both, but mostly Hell."

"Ok. That's what I thought. Have you read the chapters about Sodom and Gomorrah in the Bible, and do you know the history behind them?"

"Yeah, when I was a teenager, but I don't know about the history part."

"Well Ali, what did you think about it? Not what did others tell you it was about, but what YOU thought about it."

"Actually…I thought if the other people in the village were more hospitable that none of that would have ever happened like that. Religion is a double-edged sword to me. One passage says "Sin will not enter", but how is it possible to have absolutely no sin?"

"Ahh, so basically you have your mind made up about the religion aspect of it. Did you feel conviction when you were sleeping with her?"

"Never. Sarah made me feel whole, loved, and perfect."

"If you didn't feel it was wrong then why do you now?"

Ali thought for a minute. "I just know what everybody else says."

"You mean your family and friends?" Deanna was digging deep.

"Yeah, I guess so."

"Do you think it's fair that you live your life according to how THEY feel? Is that gonna make YOU happy?"

Ali looked down at the floor. Had she always lived her life to suit others? Is that why she was so unhappy? She wasn't being fair to herself. "Wow...I'm not even livin' my own life."

"Now you're thinking."

"So...is it possible that I have always been gay and just didn't know?"

"Only you know how you feel about this Sarah, or any man, or any other woman. You're the only one that can answer that but please research the history of the times when the stories were written in the Bible. That will give you some answers also."

Ali went home and re-read the passages of Sodom and Gomorrah. It sounded like it was all about how the angels were treated, like it had nothing to do with sexuality itself. She was happy that times were different now. She would've hated for her father to give her to a group of men to be raped repeatedly. The weird part is even though he was willing to do that Lot was spared. Ali's thoughts were so confused that she decided to take Deanna's advice and research the history behind the tales.

Over the course of two days she read articles and watched many documentaries about the Bible and homosexuality. One documentary in particular was called *For The Bible Tells Me So*. She found it on Netflix. It told the stories of several people who had grown up in the church, yet were gay. Some of them were pastor's kids. One of them even became the first openly gay cardinal.

Acclaimed and published historians told the stories of what was going on behind the scenes when the passages about Sodom and Gomorrah were written. Apparently God had already decided to destroy the cities, because they had a law that allowed no strangers in town. They didn't want to share their possessions with anyone and became cold-hearted toward their fellow mankind. They were possessive and not willing to lend a hand to those in need. Therefore, when Lot allowed two strangers into his home it angered them, and they demanded to talk to them and get to know them. They wanted to make sure that their valuables would not be taken. There was also an article about the scripture, "A man shall not sleep with a man, as he does a woman." At that time God wanted the world to be populated, and that is why he wanted the men and women to sleep together, purely for population. To prove his point he struck down Onan who refused to impregnate his brother's wife because the child would be his brother's offspring instead of his own. He slept with his sister-in-law and then spilled his seed on the ground instead of inside her, and he was struck by a bolt of lightning. Besides those facts, there were literally only 6 implications in the entire Bible that people use to go against homosexuality. In fact, the word "homosexuality" wasn't even in the Bible until placed there in 1946. She also read all of Jesus' teachings and realized that he never once spoke of anything to do with homosexuality.

Ali didn't understand the Bible. It had been re-written so many times, what was the actual truth? She decided from now on to do what felt right to her. If she felt bad about doing something then she wouldn't do it anymore. She didn't feel bad about loving Sarah anymore.

The feelings deep inside were telling her that it was natural and holy, because it made her feel so good, but she decided to talk to her mom too.

"Mom I see you've re-arranged the livin' room." Ali was trying to be engaging.

"Yep, well I figured it was about time. Your dad's been gone for over a year now, and I always did it the way he wanted it, so now I've got it my way." Betty seemed to be in a good mood, which was rare over the past year. Ever since Robert died she had some good days but mostly bad days. She was shaped like an hourglass. That's where Ali had gotten her figure from. Betty was cutting up a red ripe tomato.

"It looks nice. I have a question for ya." Ali was terrified but needed to find out her stance on lesbian relationships.

"Ok, well the answer is either yes or no." Betty's green eyes smiled at her daughter playfully.

"No it's gonna be somethin else. It's about, um, gay rights."

"Oh...why do you want to know about that?" Betty had never discussed gay rights with Ali.

Ali hesitated. "Well I found out one of the girls at the bank is a lesbian, and it got me to thinkin'."

"Oh. Did you hear about that church in North Carolina that won't marry straight couples anymore, until gay couples can get married," Betty asked?

"Huh, a church?" Ali was very interested.

"Yeah. Well where do you stand on it honey?"

"Momma...I really don't know. I think everybody deserves to be happy, and gays are definitely accepted more these days, but what about hell?"

"Hell? Have you read the Bible?! You need to re-read Sodom and Gomorrah. I think it was about the town's unhospitable nature or wantin' to have sex with the angels, you know, celestial bein's, and not about sex with other men. They had each other for that. Is this because of what your daddy always said about gays and hell? Because your daddy and me disagreed on lots of things and that was one of 'em. I happen to think hell is when you don't find the one you're supposed to be with honey. God knows your Aunt Debbie won't agree, but I believe gay, straight, blacks, whites, purples, whatever, should be allowed to marry each other. I mean if a woman overseas can marry a damn dolphin then why can't men and women marry each other?"

"Really?" Ali was in shock. She thought for sure that her mom would be against it.

"Yeah, why?"

This was her chance. She could tell her mom now. It was now or never. "I...uh...well I".

She was cut off. "You slept with her didn't ya?" Betty's eyebrows jumped up and down.

Ali's face turned red. She wanted to scream no, but she had to tell her the truth. "Uh, yeah I did."

"Lesbians are great in bed aren't they?" Betty smiled devilishly.

"You mean? You were with a woman too?"

"Oh honey, you have to realize I grew up in the sixties and seventies. Swingin' and sleepin' around was common, yes, even in Georgia. We were looked down on by some people but we were livin', ya know?"

"Wow, I, uh, so you and daddy were swingers?" Ali couldn't believe it. Her dad was always so religious, and her mom was so subservient and quiet.

"Well, just until you were born. Deanna's got you thinkin' huh?"

"Wait, so I could've been talkin' to you about this the whole time?"

"The whole time? I think you better start tellin' me what's goin on young lady!" Betty sat down in the chair right beside Ali, and gave her full attention.

Ali proceeded to tell her everything. She told her about how she yearned for Sarah but was afraid of what others were going to say, especially her. Betty wrapped her arms around Ali's neck. "You can always tell me anything. I was hopin' we'd get closer since your daddy is gone and it's just us now."

"Mom, I'd love that." Ali cried into her mother's shoulder.

"Honey, you have to find your bliss. If you know where it is, I say go after it. I just want you to be happy, and screw 'em if "they" don't like it. You're the one who has to live with yourself, not them."

"Thank you so much." Ali was relieved.

"You didn't need my permission. You needed your own. It's obvious you love her, and hey, you can work at a different bank if ya get fired."

Ali pulled away from the hug. "I love you mom." Ali smiled a besmirched grin.

11

Ali felt a confidence she hadn't felt since the first night she was raped by Mr. Loverboy. She immediately texted Sarah. "*I told my mom about us. She's supportin' me.*"

"*Really? That's great. So what now?*" She was afraid to get too excited.

"*I wanna c u.*" Ali wanted to ravage Sarah's body.

"*I wanna c u 2, but what if ur friends c us 2gether?*"

"*I don't care anymore.*" Ali just wanted to be with Sarah.

"*Ok, y dont u cum 2 my house 4 a change?*"

"*Ok, b there n 15 mins.*"

"*K.*"

Ali had a smile on her face so bright that it could have jump started the sun. Her heart felt as if it were going to explode out of her chest. She was light-headed and giddy. Sarah's neighborhood was nicer than hers. The houses were big and old, but restored to their former glory. Most of them were two stories tall. Sarah's was the simplest one on the lane. It was a big, single level, brick house; it was twice the size of Ali's. She could see Sarah's Buick in the driveway and she felt like a school girl seeing her crush for the first time.

As she pulled in to Sarah's driveway she got a text message from Sarah. "*Come on n, the door is open.*" Ali's smile got bigger with anticipation.

She pushed open the door and heard Lady Gaga's "Paparazzi" playing. As she made her way through the house she smelled vanilla. Her nose sent signals to her body causing her to crave Sarah's touch. She couldn't wait to get her hands on Sarah. She walked around the corner, into the bedroom. There were candles lit all around the room. "Sarah?"

"I'm in here baby." Her voice was coming from the master bathroom.

Ali gulped, thinking of what she was about to find. She hoped Sarah would be naked on the other side of the wall. She peered around the door frame. Sarah was in the garden tub, covered by bubbles. Her shoulders and neck were glistening by the light of the candles. Her hair was up in a hair clip. She looked very feminine. Her bare neck looked inviting to Ali's lips. Ali started breathing faster.

"Join me baby." Sarah was enthralled by Ali's heaving chest, and couldn't wait to make love to her.

Ali licked her lips, and then disrobed. Sarah stood up and offered her hand for Ali to hold while she stepped in to the tub. Ali grabbed Sarah's hand, and then looked her up and down. Sarah was glistening all over now, with a few places still covered in bubbles.

"Mmm, you look good."

Sarah smiled. "So do you baby, now come in so we can hold each other."

Ali slowly stepped in. They sat down together. Ali laid her head on Sarah's shoulder. Ali felt like she'd come back home. The world began to make sense again. The void in her heart was getting smaller. She longingly looked up at Sarah's luscious mouth, and licked her lips again. Sarah stroked Ali's hair, then bent down and kissed her hard. Their passionate kissing made the bubbles part between them. Ali saw Sarah's exposed breasts, and cupped one of them, while squeezing its nipple between her fingers. Sarah gasped. "You've still got the touch." Sarah reached under the water to caress Ali's side.

"Oh baby…there are so many things I wanna do to you. I just wanna play all over your body." Ali wanted to touch and lick every inch of Sarah.

"Mmm, well let's hurry up and get outta here." Sarah had waited months for this to happen.

They got up and out. They dried each other off. They made their way to the canopy bed. The candles were still flickering. Their shadows danced on the wall as they kissed and wrapped their arms around each other. Sarah playfully pushed Ali down on the bed. Ali sat up. "No. I want you to lie down." She pulled Sarah down beside her. Sarah didn't know what to think.

"Yes ma'am", she whispered.

Ali began by running her fingertip from Sarah's neck to her belly button. She thought of how Mr. Loverboy had been so gentle and loving with her, and she wanted to do the same thing to Sarah. Ali straddled Sarah's hips, grinding her lightly haired snatch into Sarah's. Sarah's legs spread wide. Ali leaned down and kissed Sarah's mouth, and then licked her nipples. She ran her tongue down Sarah's stomach and over her inner thighs. Sarah moaned. Ali was getting excited by the smell of Sarah's lady parts. She plunged her tongue into it. She licked up and down and then back and forth across her clit. She licked the length of Sarah's moist lips. Juices began to trickle out. About forty-five minutes had passed before her jaw was getting tired. Then she stuck her hand inside Sarah and waved her fingers back and forth. She put her whole hand inside of Sarah and pushed it hard, while rubbing her clitoris with her thumb. Sarah let out a guttural, "Ahh". This time Ali knew she liked it and hadn't hurt her, so she continued. The suction sounds of Sarah's vagina were making little spurts of cum drip from Ali. She was so turned on that she instinctively began performing oral sex on Sarah again.

Sarah's entire body jerked and bounced up and down off the bed, and her toes curled and popped. Sarah was so tired that she felt like a water puddle, moving with every shake of movement from the bed. She had several clitoral orgasms and one big vaginal orgasm. Butterflies formed in her stomach, but from relaxing body muscles, not nerves. She'd never let anyone get to her the way that Ali did. Ali had just over-taken her completely, and she allowed herself to lose control of her own body, emotions, and thoughts. Sarah was recuperating while Ali nuzzled into her shoulder and rubbed her boobs.

In a breathy, raspy, hoarse voice, Sarah said, "Oh my God! You really let yourself get into it that time. You're incredible baby."

"Hehehe. I loved it. You taste like vanilla, and now the smell of vanilla turns me on." In the middle of that sentence a thought struck her. Sarah's voice sounded like Mr. Loverboy's when he'd whispered to her hoarsely.

"Mmm good. Scientists have proven that the brain remembers smells and associates certain things with them. That's why you get turned on when you smell vanilla. I smell like vanilla, and obviously, I turn you on."

Ali was confused but decided Sarah couldn't possibly be her rapist because she didn't have a penis and because her eyes weren't hazel green. "Hey, uh, where were you that night before I called you? You know, the night you came over and I was naked?"

"Um, let's see, that was a Tuesday…oh, I went out with the girls. Why?"

"Oh, I was just wondering."

Sarah looked at Ali with a confused expression on her face. Then she jumped up off the bed and said, "Well I'm gonna go back and get in the tub. You wanna join me?"

"Sure, just give me a few minutes." Ali couldn't shake the thought that Sarah could be her rapist. She watched as Sarah disappeared into the bathroom. She sat on the edge of the bed, thinking. What if it was Sarah? Did Sarah start the whole affair by raping her? She only had the courage to make a move on Sarah because of the rape. What if she wasn't really gay, for real? But she longed for Sarah's touch, smell, skin, passion, thoughts, dreams…everything. Maybe she really was gay and Sarah had just opened her eyes to it…by raping her, gently. "I gotta know for sure." As soon as she heard Sarah sit down in the tub she jogged to her top drawer. She rifled through it quickly. There were lots of female boxers in there but also some lacy panties. She also found a strap-on, a mask, and a small container for contacts. There was the proof right in front of her. "Mr. Loverboy" was Sarah, the whole time. That night she'd smelled her own vagina because she was near Sarah's face, not because she was so turned on by her. She didn't know how to feel. She walked to the doorway of the bathroom. Sarah was leaned back with a smile on her face.

"I know it was you." Ali had to say something.

"What baby?" Sarah appeared very relaxed.

Sarah's naive act was angering Ali. "You raped me!"

Sarah stood straight up and jumped over the side of the tub. She ran to Ali, wet and shiny. "I never hurt you! I made love to you!"

"Why Sarah? Why didn't you just make a move, as yourself? What? Are you not as confident in yourself as you try to act? I mean, what's the deal?"

Tears were streaming down Sarah's face. Desperately, she pleaded, "Please don't be mad. I just knew if I tried anything you would've disappeared on me, and then I wouldn't have you in my life at all, and I was goin' crazy to touch you."

"Well, ya got what you wanted." Ali got dressed, and then left.

Tears were streaming down Ali's face. She was consciously trying not to speed home. Her phone rang and she assumed it was Sarah, so she didn't answer it. She didn't know what to say to her right now. A minute later a beep came from the phone, letting her know she had a voicemail. She waited to check it until she got home.

"Ali, this is Sharla Williams. Justin had a wreck tonight and I thought you'd want to know. (Sharla began sobbing.) The doctors aren't sure if my baby is gonna live. Please come. I know he'd want to see ya."

Ali felt horrified. The last thing she said to him was that he was a kind man and would be a good husband to someone else. Oh my God. Was this her fault? First Sarah, now Justin. What a night! Tears wouldn't stop flowing down her face.

The hospital still looked cold and boring. The waiting room was full. She called Sharla back to let her know she was there. Sharla sent the nurse out to get her.

"Ali?"

Ali turned to see Denise standing in the door way leading to the emergency room. Ali sighed. She walked over to the door. She whispered, "I see you all over the place now don't I?"

Denise smiled. "Is that such a bad thing?"

"Right now yes." She scowled at Denise.

Denise rolled her eyes. "So this is your boyfriend huh? What does your girlfriend think of this?"

"She doesn't know yet." Ali was getting angry. "Just take me back will ya!?"

Denise motioned for her to come through the door.

Ali was at her wits end. Her tact filter was bent. "Yeah, well Sarah feels sorry for ya cause ya gotta hide who ya are. I feel sorry for Deon. You got her twisted around your little finger and you're just usin' her."

"Shut up! You don't know what it's like to have to hide because your whole family will disown ya. Or how bad ya feel to be married to somebody ya don't love. Or to have kids that ya don't want to hurt. You don't know me."

Ali's feelings softened. Denise was just as tormented as she was. "Actually I do understand ya, more than ya know."

Denise looked at her with sadness in her eyes. Quietly she said, "He's right in here. I hope everything works out for ya."

"Thank you." Ali watched her walk away.

Justin's room was loud. The breathing pump was whirring and popping. There was a tube taped to his face that ran down his throat. He was lying very still. Sharla sat on the other side of the bed, holding his hand and crying. Ali instantly felt despair. A lonely tear drop formed in the corner of her eye. Mrs. Williams looked up at her.

"Please, come in. Thank you for comin'." Sharla's face was pale with puffy red eyes. She looked older than Ali remembered. Her shoulder length salt and pepper hair was pulled up in a bun on the back of her head. She stood up, walked around the foot of the bed, and gently hugged Ali. "The doctors say his neck might be severed from his spinal cord. We're still waitin' on the X-rays to come back. If it is… (hysterical sobbing) he's gonna die and we'll never get to tell him good bye!"

Ali hugged her. She didn't know what to say. Reba McIntyre's song, "What Do You Say", jumped in her head. "He is a good man."

"When he told me ya'll were back together I got so happy. I always liked you better than that Heather girl he was with." She rolled her eyes.

"Actually Mrs. Williams…we broke up…how did the wreck happen?" She was so scared she was at fault.

"Oh. I didn't know. He didn't tell me that. I'm sorry I bothered ya." Sharla was offended.

"No, ya didn't bother me. I wanna be here."

"Well, why did ya break up with him then?

Ali looked down at the floor. "It's complicated."

"It's that damn woman ain't it?

Ali was flabbergasted. How did she know? "Huh?"

"Yeah I know all about your torrid little affair. Charlotte Smalley told me. I didn't have the heart to tell Justin. I knew it would hurt him."

What could she say to that? "It's not like I meant for it to happen. It just did."

"Yeah well we never mean for things to happen, do we? I'm sure ya didn't wish he'd get hit by a semi, but he did." She burst into tears again.

"I'm sorry…but at least we both know it was an accident and he didn't do it on purpose."

"Oh, I see. You thought he did this because ya broke up with him, huh?"

"Well I hoped not."

"You're full of yourself aren't ya?"

Ali's eyes were squinted together in disbelief. "No…I'm not."

"Sorry…I'm just upset. I'll give ya a few minutes alone with him ok." She turned and walked out the door.

Ali stood in place momentarily, just looking at him. He seemed so lifeless. She thought about his smile, and the way she used to crave his attention. She didn't want him to die. He was a friend, which she could use right now. She rounded the bed and sat in the chair.

"Justin I don't know if ya can hear me or not but I need to tell ya somethin'. I will always love ya. You were a part of my life for five years; I thought we'd be married at one time." She paused. "After we broke up I stayed single for a while but then I got to know somebody real good and I fell in love. It's my lesbian friend Sarah, from work." She said it out loud. It didn't sound as bad as she thought. "Well that's why I couldn't get back together with ya. I'm still in love with her. Actually, bein' with her made me realize I was never actually in love with you. I was in puppy love with you. I'm sorry. I didn't know I was gay. I would never have hurt ya on purpose. You were always good to me. I really did mean that you would be a good husband someday, and I hope you get the chance to prove it."

"Ya gotta tell her the truth. She's a keeper." Denise was standing in the doorway.

"You spyin' on me?" Ali was agitated.

"It was unintentional. I came by to check on him and just overheard ya, but ya know I'm right."

"It's not that easy Denise."

"It can be. Don't be like me. Be better. Stand up for yourself now, while you're young, before you get caught up in takin' care of others, without thinkin' about yourself."

"You can still do it ya know? EVERYbody deserves to be happy, even you."

Denise smirked. "Touché."

Ali stood up, leaned over and kissed Justin on the forehead, and left.

While Ali was at the hospital with Justin, Sarah called. Ali didn't answer so she texted. *"Baby pls cum back. It was stupid idk y I did it. Im sorry."* She got no reply. She was so upset that she decided to go out and get drunk. She threw on a pair of shorts and a tank top, and then headed to the Golden Ridge Inn.

Sarah's eyes were swollen from crying, and she felt a little dizzy but she was determined to forget Ali for the night. They played Lady Gaga, Merle Haggard, Maroon 5,

Madonna's eighties hits, and AC/DC. She started off with a Rattlesnake, and then drank six shots of tequila.

A drunken young lady, named Lisa, sat beside her. "So you're a lesbian right?" The strawberry blonde was slurring her words terribly.

"Yeah, but you're too young for me." Sarah was in no mood for the games.

"Why? You're only like thirty right?"

Sarah laughed. "Ha. Thirty-six honey. What are ya? Eighteen?"

"No! I'm twenty-one."

"Same thing. Besides I'm in love with somebody else."

"So. I just wanna fuck a woman, and you're fine. I would gladly touch you."

Sarah smiled. "I'm flattered, but no thank you."

Lisa walked away, loudly telling her friends that the "gay girl" was in love, and that they couldn't get any that night. Sarah decided to go on home, so she called a taxi. She went home and crashed in bed.

The next morning, Sarah awoke to a lawn mower running next door. Her head was pounding. She got up and took two aspirins. She realized that she hadn't even taken her shoes off the night before. She wondered what Ali was doing, so she called her. Ali didn't answer. She sent her a text. *"Pls answer me. I luv u n miss u."* She waited twenty minutes, but got no reply.

She brushed her teeth, called a cab, got her car, and then went to her mom's house. She spent the whole day talking about Ali. Raynita, Sarah's mom, listened and suggested she send flowers, candy, and a card, anything she could think of to smooth things over.

"I can't believe you raped her. You know that's wrong! The Great Spirit is disappointed, and so am I. How could you do that? You took away her choice to be with you. You forced her into something she didn't want at first. You're lucky she wanted you after that. You went about this all wrong; we need to fix it spiritually."

Sarah listened intently, and respectfully did what her mother asked. "Momma I know you're right. Will you help me? I need help." They spent the next few hours praying for forgiveness and performing rituals to bring peace back to Sarah and Ali's relationship.

Ali visited her mom Saturday also. Betty was in a good mood again.

"Mom we need to talk."

"That sounds serious honey."

"It's very serious."

"Justin was in a wreck last night and I don't know if he's gonna make it. I feel bad about it though because I broke up with him."

"Aww. I'm sorry baby. I know he was an important part of your life. Death is an unfortunate side effect of life. If he does die you still have the memories he left with ya, which is what ya would have had anyhow since ya broke up. You had said good bye to him emotionally already. Now you're gonna have to do it physically. Sometimes it hits ya harder than the emotional stuff, because it's final and absolute. Just look at it as if he will be out of pain, and in a better state. Now…what's goin' on with Sarah?"

"Oh god. Sarah is Mr. Loverboy!"

"What! You mean all this time and it's been her?! How?"

"Momma…it was a strap-on."

"Wow…I guess she really wanted to be with ya." She stressed to find the right words to say. "At least she got to know ya before she slept with ya. So it's not just physical." She was trying to comfort Ali.

"What are ya sayin'? I should just forgive her and go on with life, with her?"

"I can't tell ya that. Ya have to figure that out on your own honey. I guess…it depends on how much ya love her, and how much she loves you."

"I don't know exactly what to do, but something's gotta change."

Monday came and they hadn't had any communication. Ali received text messages from Sarah but didn't respond. She wasn't sure about what she wanted to say yet.

Sarah always got to the bank before Ali, so they were looking for each other around seven forty-five. Ali noticed Sarah staring at her as she walked in. Sarah noticed right away that Ali's hair had been cut in a pixie style. Ali passed her office, looking down. Sarah stepped out of her door and watched Ali clock in. Ali was wearing a flowered skirt, high heels, a sleeveless shirt, and with the new do she looked like a completely new person. Ali was stunningly gorgeous. Sarah continued to watch as she walked over to the counter to take her work position. Sarah walked over to the other side of the counter, and stood right in front of Ali. Ali looked up into Sarah's eyes.

"You look great, fantastic even."

"Thank you Ms. Buckman. I thought it was time for a change." She jerked her head to the side to make her hair flow backward, but it didn't move. She forgot it wasn't long enough to do that anymore.

Sarah wasn't used to Ali calling her by her last name. She was so impersonal that Sarah sulked back to her office.

Ali glanced as Sarah walked away. She was wearing Ali's favorite power suit. It was navy blue, with white pin stripes, and she wore a silky white tie. Her muscular thighs stretched the pants in just the right way, and her round bottom was accentuated by the fitted fabric.

The bank was unusually busy. The summer sun brought out everyone and their brother. Sarah and Ali stared at each other often. Then they left to go to lunch at the same time.

Once they were outside the bank, Sarah called out for Ali. She turned and looked at her. "Would you like to go to lunch with me Ms. Carter?"

"Thanks, but no thanks. I have plans already. I'm seein' Justin, and I have a job interview."

Sarah was in awe. Her gut did a flip-flop. She was about to lose Ali forever. Sadly she said, "Oh, well good luck."

Sarah's mind was running through anything she could think of to keep Ali working there. She came back from lunch early. She was too upset to eat anyhow. She got on the phone and ordered flowers and candy, signed, "Mr. Loverboy". They would be delivered within the hour; hopefully before Ali got back.

Six long-stem roses were waiting at Ali's station when she returned from her job interview. She couldn't wait to read the card. As she rounded the counter she looked into Sarah's office. Sarah was staring at her. She read the card, and then glanced over at Sarah. She was still staring. Ali mouthed the words, "thank you". Sarah smiled.

The other girls inquired as to who Mr. Loverboy was. Ali just smiled. "Wouldn't you like to know?"

Erica Smalley walked over to Ali and said, "I bet I know."

Ali looked at her inquiringly. "You have a big mouth."

"It's not a he, is it?"

Ali guffawed. "What! Are you crazy?"

"No, I'm not." She leaned in and whispered in Ali's ear. "It's her isn't it? Sarah."

Ali quickly looked at Sarah, then back at Erica. Quietly she said, "No".

"It's okay ya know. We all know. We've seen how ya'll look at each other. And we also know ya'll are fightin' right now. You were so happy, then Justin showed up and ya got sad again. Ya look like you're goin' through somethin' big right now. Its Justin isn't it? I'm sorry I didn't think it would bother ya so bad. Ya know…'cause ya'll broke up. Do ya need to talk?"

Ali was befuddled. She didn't know what to say. "Ya mean, ya'll have known this whole time, and not treated me any different, and what about Justin? We're still friends."

"Why would we? You're just gay. It's not like you're a killer…He died this morning. Ya didn't know?"

"What…no, I didn't know. I was just about to go see him but I ran out of time. I…wow…so everybody knows about me?" She looked around at the other girls. They were all smiling at her. She felt a warm sensation in her heart. She felt acceptance and disappointment at the same time.

"Yep and we've been waitin' for ya to "come out" but you didn't tell anybody. Well, everybody except Beulah. She's been sayin you're goin' to hell, but we don't listen to her anyhow. She's just old."

"Well I was, scared. Justin is really gone?"

"Listen girlie, you gotta let your freak flag fly, whatever it is, and we want ya to be happy again…Yeah, he is."

Ali's eyes watered. She fought back the tears. Sarah saw her and immediately knew something was wrong. She sent her a text message. *"R u ok? Y r u cryin?"*

Ali replied, *"Justin died."*

"Oh shit. Im sorry."

Sarah looked back at Ali. She was hugging Erica. She didn't know what to do or say. She wanted to be the one hugging Ali, but knew it wouldn't be right. They both had to worry about their jobs, well she did. Obviously Ali wanted to go somewhere else.

A few minutes later she saw Ali leave. Sarah was left feeling awful, not knowing what to do, although she felt as though she should do something. She pulled out her phone and texted Ali. *"I'm here 4 u always."* She received no reply. Ali wasn't at work the next two days and she wouldn't answer Sarah's texts or phone calls.

Ali had a few black dresses, but she couldn't decide which one to wear. The past few days had been just sad and lonely. Her eyes were constantly watering. Justin was an important person to her. He was a decent friend but he'd taught her so much about herself. If she couldn't be with a man as good as Justin then she obviously didn't want to be with men at all. He treated her with respect though and so she knew how she wanted to be treated. She wanted to call Sarah, and see her, and hold her. On the other hand she felt like she shouldn't get close to anyone again. It hurt too much to lose someone you love, and she'd already lost her one time. She figured she'd just be alone.

The funeral was gloomy and Sharla was so depressed. Mr. Williams was stoic. His face seemed carved out of stone, but his eyes told a different story. They looked weak. Mr. and Mrs. Williams no longer had a child on the earth. They would forever be changed, and so would she. She'd always remember Justin's kind spirit and smile. On the car ride home she put in her Ozzy Ozborne CD. It comforted her in her sadness. That afternoon she spent a few hours looking at pictures of her and Justin, and remembering their time together.

A knock came at the door. She wiped her face, pulled her robe closed, and answered the door.

"Ali. This is from Justin. It was found in his car when the cops cleaned it out." Sharla was holding an envelope. She pushed it toward Ali. Ali reached out and accepted it. Sharla squeezed her hand. "I want ya to pay attention to his last words, and take them to heart."

"You read it?" Ali was hurt.

"Yes. I'm sorry, but I had to know what he was thinkin' before he left us."

Ali could understand that. "Oh."

"Just do what he asks. Let him have his last wish. Please." Sharla wiped her tears away and quickly stepped off of her steps and walked to her car.

Ali looked at the envelope again. She was curious about it. Was this about to make her wish she'd never broken up with him? Why did she have to feel bad about it for so long?

My dearest Ali,

Our lives sure haven't turned out the way we planned. I wish you the best, even though it won't be with me. It's obvious to me that you are in love. I can tell because I remember the look you used to give me when you were in love with me. Thank you for giving me those years. I wish I hadn't been a fool and let you go. You were always good to me, and for that I want to thank you as well. I only want to see you happy. That's my number one wish because you are my number one. You're the love of my life and always will be. That's why I want you to be happy no matter what. You deserve to be happy. Yes, I wish it could be with me, but I know I don't want you to be in a relationship you're not happy with. I love you enough to let you go. Please, go forth and live the life you want. Do it in memory of our once perfect love, and because you deserve it. I love you now and always will.

Yours forever,

Justin

Williams

Allison broke down. Her knees buckled under her and she cried right there on the front steps. She didn't realize he felt so intensely for her. He didn't act like it, or did he? Maybe he thought he was showing it. Maybe that was his best. If so, then why wasn't it enough for her? He was a good man, and cute. His smile was contagious, even on the worst day. He was kind, a hard worker, and he was a social butterfly. He had so many good points but she still didn't want to be with him. Why? Maybe she didn't have the best capabilities when it came to picking someone to love. She wanted to be held by Sarah. It was all she wanted. That was her one wish at the moment; and what about Sarah? How would she be able to love her knowing that she had messed Justin's world up so bad? Maybe she just wasn't girlfriend material. Maybe she should just be asexual. Then nobody gets hurt or disappointed, except her.

She couldn't escape from thoughts of Sarah's loving arms. She needed to feel loved and appreciated, by someone who was alive. Even though Sarah had "raped" her as Mr. Loverboy she still wanted her. Her life seemed to be in turmoil. She didn't know which way to turn. Justin's death had her feeling kind of numb toward life. She wanted to feel alive. She really missed Sarah. She rubbed across her own nipple. It stood at attention. She imagined that Sarah was touching her. She became aroused. Her panties were moist. She pinched her nipples and pulled them. A knot formed in the pit of her stomach. She softly moaned. The bed was seductively holding her in its grasp. She ran her finger down the middle of her stomach. Her nipples stayed hard. She slid her foot up to her bottom so that she could open her vagina easily. She slid her hand down inside of her panties. With her middle finger she caressed her clitoris. She did it faster and harder and it only took two minutes to come. When she was done she wiped her hand on her panties and then flipped over on her side, snuggling with a body pillow. She quietly cried. Justin died, and she didn't have Sarah. She was afraid to. What if something happened to her? She wouldn't be able to handle it.

<u>12</u>

A month had gone by, and Ali had only said hello to Sarah. She was too afraid to get attached to her, so she isolated herself. She only saw her mother and brother. She was afraid to have any fun because Justin was dead. How would it look if she were out having fun? She was depressed.

"Honey, you've got to get back out there. Justin is dead, not you."

"Mom, that's a terrible thing to say." Ali couldn't believe her ears.

Betty shook her head. "No, it's the truth. You're still alive. You have a life to lead. You can't let one death throw off your whole life. As you get older more and more people ya know are gonna die. How are ya gonna handle that?"

Ali looked down at the floor. "But it wasn't just anybody who died."

Betty wrapped her arms around Ali's waist and hugged her. "I know Pumpkin. I was with your dad for thirty-six years. Trust me I know what it's like to lose someone important."

Ali suddenly realized how selfish she was being. She only knew Justin for about ten years. He was an important part of her life but he was gone. "Momma, I don't want to be unhappy anymore." Ali cried into her mother's neck.

Betty pulled away from the hug. "You don't have to be. In fact he wanted you be to be happy. Remember the letter? You have to love yourself as much as he loved ya. He knew you were in love with Sarah, well with somebody else. Do you realize what a sacrifice he made so that you could be happy?"

"What are ya talkin' about?"

"Ali he loved you and wanted you for himself, but his love for you was stronger than his desires. That's how he was able to let ya go."

Ali cried gently. "But I didn't want his love." She looked down at the floor, as if she were ashamed.

Betty reached over and sweetly lifted Ali's chin, until they were looking at each other. "Honey, what you're not seein' is all he wanted was for YOU to have that same feeling toward somebody; to love somebody so deeply that their happiness comes before yours." Betty cleared her throat. "He saw that potential in the relationship that you were yearnin' for. I see it too, ya know?"

"Ya mean, with Sarah?" Ali thought hard about that. "I really do care about her, not just physically. I want her to be happy and satisfied with life. I want her to have everything she's lookin' for. I want her to...well, I just want her." Ali looked at her mom. "Is that such a bad thing?"

"It's only bad if you see the relationship goin' nowhere. There is no reason to get back into it if you don't think it has potential. Otherwise you're wastin' her time and yours." Ali thought her mom was right. Of course she wouldn't tell her that.

The next day at work she received a bouquet of flowers. The card was unsigned. It simply said, "Always". Ali looked at Sarah and smiled. Sarah smiled back. That word always had a lot of meaning to it. It wasn't a word to just be thrown around lightly. Always was a long time, and encompassed the good and the bad. Did Sarah feel for her the way that Justin had? Why did she suddenly decide to reach out?

Sarah sent more varieties of flower arrangements to Ali; one for each day of the week. She also sent her sweet text messages, and called and left sweet messages on her voicemail. Sarah had been a mess this last month. She was depressed but tried to keep up the appearance that everything was alright. She knew that Ali needed time to work through her emotions for Justin, and the fact that he was dead. She wanted to wrap her arms around Ali, every day, but she knew she had to fight the urges. She'd even thought of going to Ali's house as Mr. Loverboy, but decided that would probably be inappropriate. She wanted to contact her outside of work, but really didn't know what to say. She knew she'd messed up by being Mr. Loverboy, but Ali was actually smiling at her again. Maybe Ali could love her again.

They stared at each other all week at work. Every day when Ali would get flowers she would smile at Sarah. She thought the action of sending flowers each day was a grand romantic gesture. The card said "I'm yours," on Tuesday. Wednesday the card read, "Today and forever." The card read, "I want you back," on Thursday. Friday the card read, "With ALL of me."

Ali knew she was coming back to life because she felt giddy inside. She felt as though she were the love interest in a movie that has a happy ending. As each day passed she was overcome by emotions. Finally she decided it was time to make Sarah and herself happy. She couldn't stand the distance anymore.

Ali texted Sarah. *"Will u meet me @ the Inn on Tues? We need 2 talk."*

"I can meet u anytime, even 2day." Sarah hoped Ali would want to see her before Tuesday.

"Tues will b good. 8 pm."

"Ok." Sarah longed for Ali to talk to her, face to face, instead of through texts. Now she had to worry about what Ali was going to say.

Ali had to figure out what to say to Sarah, but she also worried about Sarah's response. The next few days drug by slowly. Sarah wanted to see Ali, and Ali wanted to see Sarah, but Ali was calling the shots right now, and she needed space to figure some things out.

Sarah's mind was again running rampant thinking about what Ali was going to tell her that night. It was driving her crazy not to know what was going on. She was thinking the worst possible thoughts. Was Ali moving away? Was she never coming out of the closet? Was she getting another job just so she wouldn't have to see her every day? Would she ever see her again after Tuesday?

Finally, it was Tuesday, and quitting time. Sarah went straight to McDonalds and got two McChickens and a sweet tea, and then headed home. She ate in a hurry, and then hopped in the tub. Sarah wanted to make sure that she was fresh and clean. She shaved her legs, underarms, and labia. Shaving always made her feel sexy. After her bath, Sarah put on her favorite lotion and body spray; warm vanilla – the kind that turns Ali on. She straightened her hair and put on eye shadow, which she hadn't done in months. Normally she didn't wear make-up but she was willing to do anything that could possibly help the situation tonight. She carefully selected the outfit that Ali had once said was "really hot" on her. It was a baby blue tank top and a pair of khaki shorts. Ali had told her that the colors complimented her skin perfectly. She slid on her white New Balance tennis shoes and then sat down to watch TV. There was still an hour and a half left before she was to meet Ali at eight o'clock. Sarah sat on her bed worrying again, about what Ali was going to tell her.

Ali was eager about meeting Sarah. She went straight home from work and made a tuna salad sandwich, then got in the shower. She shaved her legs, underarms, and vagina also. She smeared mousse in her hair to hold it in place. She applied eyeliner and lathered up with cucumber melon lotion. She was anxious to face the night. She was afraid of what would happen because she didn't know how Sarah would react to her news. However, she did know she wanted to pick out something that would make Sarah wish they were still together. Ali combed through her closet and chose a red leather mini skirt that she'd never worn and a black tank top. Afterwards she tried on several pairs of shoes before settling on a pair of shiny black pumps. Ali painted her toenails a bright red. She felt confident in her look. She sat down on her couch and watched TV, to pass the time away.

Ali's heart was pounding fast as she drove to meet Sarah. She looked around to see if Sarah's car was there and she didn't see it. Ali took a deep breath, reminded herself that she had to say it, and went in, after checking herself one last time in the mirror.

Sarah pulled up and scanned the parking lot. Ali's car was already there. She combed her hair and popped in a breath mint. She tried to remain calm, but she was almost ready to text Ali and tell her she couldn't make it. She thought if she didn't hear the words that it couldn't be happening, but then made herself go in. As she walked through the parking lot toward the building, she noticed that there were three other cars that looked familiar. Sarah hadn't thought about the fact that it was a Tuesday night and the other girls would be there. She cautiously continued to stride on. Even if she had to make a fool of herself she was going in to see Ali.

The room was dimly lit. Sarah could make out banners in the darkness, but she couldn't tell what they said. The dance floor inhabited several couples, all of whom turned to look at her when she opened the front door. The females of the couples smiled at her politely then looked back at their dance partners. Sarah's eyes searched the room for Ali. She was sitting at a table alone, picking her nails. Ali looked as anxious as Sarah felt. Suddenly, Sarah's stomach began doing summer saults. Her nerves were worked up again. Ali lifted her eyes to Sarah's and sat up high in her chair, and then tugged on her tank top so it would cover her stomach properly. Slowly, Sarah made her way across the bar. She noticed how beautiful Ali appeared. She was glowing. Her outfit was sexy, and the heels plus the red nail polish were hot. Her hair was perfectly in place.

"Hey pretty lady. Feel like gettin' some tonight?" Lisa had stepped in her path. Sarah gave her a look of disgust and walked around her, toward Ali.

"Hello gorgeous," Sarah greeted Ali.

"Heller," replied Ali, playfully imitating Madea.

Sarah smiled, and then sat down across from Ali. "You look really pretty tonight."

"Oh my God! You're wearin' make-up. You look so good."

"Thanks babe. So…?" Sarah glanced around the room, spotting Erica Smalley. "They're here too? Oh shit. Your cover is gonna be blown."

Ali smiled, looking down at the floor. "I, uh, wanted to talk to you about somethin' important."

Sarah gulped. This was the moment of truth. Was Ali out of her life for good?

"Sarah…I'm..."

"What!" Sarah couldn't contain her emotions.

"Calm down!" She took a deep breath. "Well, ya know I, I'm…pregnant."

Sarah was shocked. "Well, I, uh, wow, I don't know what to say baby. Are you okay, I mean, happy?"

"You called me baby…do you still love me?"

Sarah's voice softened. "You know it."

"Even with a baby on the way?" Ali was scared that Sarah wouldn't want to have anything to do with her anymore.

"Even if you were a murderer…I already told you I love all of you, and I meant that."

"I…I wish…that you…were…the daddy. I don't know how the baby will feel growin' up without one. I don't even know how I feel about it really. Besides, you would be better for the baby."

Sarah's eyes teared up. "Wait. You mean you do wanna be with me?"

"Oh my God, YES! I do, so bad. I know…that what you did was wrong but it opened my world up to who I really am. For Christ's sake, I'd still be livin' in a sad, sad closet if not for you."

"Are you "out"?"

Ali looked down at her watch. "What time is it?"

"Huh?" Sarah was more than a little confused.

"Hold on. I'll be back in two minutes." Ali quickly walked away from the table.

Sarah watched as her buttocks swished back and forth, and then disappeared around the corner to the pool room. She looked around the bar. She didn't see Erica or any of the other girls. Something strange was going on.

Sarah waited patiently. Suddenly Monya came running out of the pool room, barreling at Sarah. "Come quick, he got her."

The urgent tone in her voice made Sarah react immediately. She sprang up and ran to the pool room. The back door was open. Erica Smalley was just outside on the step. She pointed toward tail lights and said, "He took her off in that truck. It's a black F-350."

"Call Officer Sparks! Now!" Sarah darted across the parking lot and into her vehicle. She sped down the road to catch up with the truck.

"Davey slow down!" Ali was scared.

"I told ya. I told ya I'd be back!"

"Please don't hurt me; I'm pregnant, with your baby." Sarah tried to deter him from violence.

"Sure ya are." He thought she was lying.

"I really am. I'm two and a half months along." She grabbed ahold of the bar above her right shoulder. He was driving erratically. "I swear it! Feel my belly if ya don't believe me."

He looked over at her in disbelief. He reached out his right hand and placed it on her stomach. It was hard. "How do I know this isn't a trick?"

She knew his walls were coming down,' and a sense of confidence spilled out. "Right! Because I knew when I left the house tonight I would run into you."

He slowed the truck down and pulled over on the grassy ditch. "Let me feel it again."

Ali lifted her shirt. She guided his hand across the hardest part of her stomach. "See? That's our baby."

Headlights flashed in the rearview mirror. Sarah had finally caught up to them.

"Let me guess…that's your girlfriend?"

Ali snapped her head backwards to look out the back window. Sarah's Buick was sitting about twenty feet behind them. She was afraid of what might happen. She yelled out the open window. "I'm fine!"

Police sirens rang out in the night. Davey pulled a gun out of his waist line. He looked at Ali. "I'm not goin' to jail." He rested the gun on the top of the circular steering wheel. "Get out. Take care of my baby."

Ali quickly scrambled out of the truck and into the deepest part of the ditch. Slowly she crawled toward Sarah's car. She heard two police cars pull up. She heard them yell freeze, and then they instructed Davey to get out slowly with his hands up. As she got to the tire of Sarah's car she jolted up. She snuck a peek at what the cops were doing. That's when she saw Sarah scampering down the road to

Davey's truck. She loudly whispered Sara's name, but she obviously didn't hear her. She watched as Sarah gently climbed up into the back of the truck. The cops were yelling, "Nobody move!" Sarah kept going. The policemen came out from behind the car doors that they were using as shields. Their guns were still drawn and aimed at the truck. Davey was looking toward the cops and yelling, "I'm not goin' to jail."

Sarah got up to the cab and turned to put her back next to it. She was facing her own car and saw Ali crying and holding her heart. Sarah closed her eyes, took a deep breath, and then released it. "Davey."

A voice came from the back of the truck. "Who is it?"

"It's me, Sarah. Don't do this."

"You don't know me, I already told ya."

"You're gonna be a father man, a father. Just put the gun down."

"Hell no!"

"Listen…this baby is gonna need a daddy, even if he's in prison. This should give you somethin' to live for." Sarah tried to get through to him. She grew up without a father and knew she didn't want the baby to be the same way.

"I won't be part of its life anyways…ya'll would keep it from me."

"No. We won't." She looked back at Ali. Ali was crying ferociously. "If you're half the guy Ali said you used to be then you need to be there for this child. Two mommas are good but a daddy makes it better."

"Ya mean it?"

"Yeah. I do."

He put the gun out the window and dropped it on the pavement.

Sarah stood up and placed her hands in the air. She climbed down out of the truck and went to Ali. They wrapped their arms around each other and rocked back and forth. It was like time stood still. They both knew they didn't want to live without the other.

"You came to rescue me, but you ended up rescuin' him." Ali was proud of Sarah.

Sarah smiled. "There's nothin' I wouldn't do for you…even save the creep that raped ya."

Ali cried into Sarah's hair. "You really do love me don't ya?"

"With all of myself." She pulled away and kissed Ali so hard that their lips went numb.

Davey stared at them from the back of the police car. They turned and watched as they drove him away.

"We need to go back and let everyone know we're ok." Ali still wanted to go to the Golden Ridge Inn.

They held hands as they drove back to the Inn. "I love you Ali." Ali squeezed Sarah's hand tighter.

They entered and hugged all their friends. They were all happy to see them. Ali told Sarah to go back to the table. Sarah sat there for a few minutes, and then turned around to face the Deejay. Their eyes connected and he nodded hello to her. She smiled. The song changed to "Listen To Your Heart", by Roxette, and the whole place got dark. When the lights came back on, Sarah saw Ali standing in the middle of the dance floor. Ali was looking right at her. Sarah got chills. Ali motioned for Sarah to come to her side. Sarah stood up, walked over to Ali, looking only into her eyes.

Sarah whispered, "What are ya doin'? You know people can see ya."

Ali wrapped her arms around Sarah and gently began rocking back and forth. "I don't care anymore. I want you and nobody else. Look up."

Sarah was taken aback. She lifted her head to face the ceiling. The banners said, "Ali is out of the closet." Sarah darted a look at Ali, with her eyes wide open. "Oh my God! Is this for real?"

"Yes it is. The girls helped me make the banners."

"So they know about us?"

"Yeah. I told 'em."

Sarah pulled Ali closer to her and kissed her hard. They were in their own plane of existence, both of them knowing their world wouldn't be complete without the other. They also danced to "All I Wanna Do Is Make Love To You", by Heart. Their dancing was intense and sexual. Then they sat back down, side by side. There was a rectangular cake on the table, and Erica, Leslie, and Monya were standing at the corner of the table. They were all smiling.

"Were ya surprised? I've never thrown a comin' out party before." Erica was hoping they'd aided in making Sarah happy.

Sarah smiled, very brightly. "Yeah. I definitely wasn't expectin' this."

Sarah looked down at the cake. It read,"Ali is out and the door is closed."

After a few drinks the girls left Ali and Sarah alone at the table.

"I want to apologize for," she whispered, "raping you."

Ali waited a moment then responded, "I know it wasn't right, but…it opened my eyes to who I truly am. If you hadn't I don't know where I would be. Mr. Loverboy was the catalyst for my peace of mind, and…for having you."

Sarah smirked, and then grabbed Ali's hand. "I am yours, ya know, faithfully."

"Well…we have a lot to discuss. I mean what about our livin' arrangements? The baby?" Ali wanted to talk on a serious note.

"We have forever, and always, to talk about all this." She paused. She couldn't help but be excited. "So. A baby? Do you know anything about babies?"

Ali smiled. She felt content knowing that Sarah was accepting her and the baby. "Sarah, I have a younger brother."

"Yeah but you were like four when he was a baby. What could you possibly remember from back then?"

"Haha. I read a lot, plus there are videos on YouTube. What about you? Do you know anything about babies?"

"Actually I do. I love kids and they love me. I've always wanted one of my own." Sarah's eyes widened and her face spread into a smile. The thought of having a child with Ali was stupendous.

"You're full of surprises." Ali leaned over and rubbed Sarah's thigh. "I never would have pegged you as a kid person."

Sarah placed her hand on top of Ali's. "Well, I must admit, you surprised me too. I thought you were gonna leave town or somethin', and you were comin' to tell me good bye."

"Oh Sarah." Ali snuggled into her neck. "You're not as tough as you let on, are ya?"

Sarah snickered. "Well you, Ms. Thang, sure have gotten stronger."

"I guess I turned out to be a star after all." Ali smiled.

Sarah's eyes widened again. "Thank God! It was killin' me not to be with you. Are ya really gettin' another job?"

"Well yeah. That's the only way we can be together and you not lose your position. However, now that I'm pregnant I'm gonna have to wait a while."

Sarah smiled. "I love you my Starlet."

"I love you too, Mr. Loverboy."

13

Ali's phone rang. Sparks was on the line.

"Ms. Carter, are you by chance still with Ms. Buckman?"

"Yes sir I am."

"Well I need both of you ladies to come to the station so we can make a report about what happened. You left so quickly that the deputies didn't have time to catch you."

"Sorry sir, I just wanted to get away from him as soon as possible."

"I understand Ms. Carter."

"Can we come see you tomorrow? We both need rest."

"Fine. Come in at nine."

"Yes sir."

"Sparks wants us at the station at nine in the morning."

"Ali…are you ok?" Sarah reached out and held her hand.

Ali's mouth crooked into a smile and a fulfilled look came over her eyes. "I am now."

That night they held each other tenderly. This time was different. They were in tune with each other. They stared into each other's eyes and shared heated kisses as Sarah gently massaged Ali's arms, legs, and feet. They spoke no words, there was no need. Sarah gleefully kissed all over Ali's body and then sucked on her nipples. Ali's vagina was thumping. Sarah ran her hands through Ali's short hair and smiled at her adoringly. Sarah then kissed Ali's stomach and swirled her tongue across Ali's labia. Ali lifted her legs and held them up. Sarah then began licking inside of Ali. She brought her to three orgasms; each one bigger than the last. Ali waved her hand to say stop, and Sarah stood up, stretched, and then lay beside her. They French kissed; rubbing each other's tongues. Ali easily rolled Sarah over on her back. She kissed Sarah's neck and sucked on it. Sarah pulled Ali closer to her. Ali then licked Sarah's nipples and suckled them. Sarah's eyes rolled back in her head. Ali went down on Sarah for a long time, curling her tongue around Sarah's clit, and suckling on it. They touched each other with confidence, sweetness, and consideration. They beamed with love; it poured off of them like hot candle wax. They both fought the tiredness that had set in on them. Their bodies were exhausted, yet they reveled in the glory of having one another. They passionately made love, with no inhibitions, for four hours. They lay naked on the bed, encompassing each other's body, as if they were one being. Ali didn't know if it was because she was so tired or because of the circumstances but she felt as though she were in a dream; one that she never wanted to wake up from.

The morning sun glared through the window. Ali looked around the room. Sarah's house was beautiful. The bedroom was like a picture from a catalog. The pillows were firm and fluffy. The sheets were satin and the comforter set was a flowery pattern colored in mauve, hunter green, and light blue. The canopy bed was romantic. The smell of food sent her into the kitchen. Sarah was making turkey bacon, egg whites, and whole grain toast.

"Good morning beautiful."

Ali smiled and rubbed her eyes. "Good morning. It smells great. Do I have time for a shower before its ready?"

"No 'cause I wanna take a shower with you." Sarah sheepishly smiled.

"Mmm. That sounds better." Ali walked up behind Sarah and wrapped her arms around her, and then kissed her neck. As she pulled her head away from Sarah she saw two little hickies. "Oh shit! You have hickies on your neck."

"Hehe. I know. I already saw 'em."

"I'm sorry. I...I didn't mean to. Now everybody is gonna know we made love all night."

Sarah turned to face Ali. "So? Are ya still worried? Most people assume lesbians have sex all the time anyhow."

"I don't know if I'm a full on lesbian or not, but I am a Sarah-bian." Ali laughed out loud.

Sarah snickered. "Well people are gonna see ya as a lesbian now anyhow, especially when we're always together."

"Well I do care a little but not like I did."

"Good Ali, 'cause I gotta tell ya, it will get easier but only if you're in the right frame of mind. Now it's not about others...it's about how you feel and act."

"What do you mean?"

"Well you'll be perceived however someone sees lesbians. It's up to you as to whether ya perpetuate that stereotype or show 'em a different kind of lesbian. I strive to always be the best person I can, and don't let the politics of my sexuality get in the way."

Ali understood that perfectly. "Gotcha."

After breakfast they cleaned up the dishes, and then showered together. They washed each other's hair and body, and then fingered each other while looking into one another's eyes. They dried each other off as well. After they were dressed, Sarah reminded Ali to call Mr. Stanley to let him know she would be late. Ali called him from her cell phone, and then Sarah called him from hers. Mr. Stanley told both of them to take the day off.

The police station was a simple two-story brick building that used to be the jail. The new jail was slightly out of town. There were ten police cars in the parking lot. Each of them had tinted windows and was white with a royal blue stripe down the side. Maverick County had just obtained new Dodge Chargers for their safety officers.

"Well there's the new car that they got through federal funds." Sarah didn't like the fact that the police officers got the cars and that the football stadium had been re-modeled to include tunnels for the players to run out onto the field from. She thought the county could have bought new books or computers for the schools, or even put in a park on the busy side of town.

"Yeah...I've already seen them." Ali wasn't impressed either.

"Do you know where we're goin'?"

"Yeah, up stairs to the left." Ali had been to his office once before.

Sarah looked up at the building. It was at least three stories but no one used the top level. It was a plain, square, brick building, surrounded by huge old oak trees. "I've only been in here once. I had to go before the judge for a speedin' ticket."

"Wow you must have been goin' pretty fast."

"Eh, seventy-two in a forty-five. The bad part is I had just turned sixteen two weeks before that."

Ali smirked. "You don't drive like that now."

"Damn straight. I learned my lesson."

The trudge up the stairs made Ali feel how much her legs were still hurting. "Ow."

"What's the matter is it the baby?" Sarah jolted around.

"No, my legs. They're sore from last night, and this morning." She smiled.

"Well baby, get used to it. I plan on makin' love to ya a lot."

At that moment a female deputy was coming down the stairs and she giggled. Ali looked down at the step she was on. She didn't want the lady to see how embarrassed she was. "Go, go, and go." She pushed Sarah up the stairs quickly.

They sat outside of Sparks' office for a few minutes and then he called them in.

"We need to get both of yall's statement so to save time I will do one and my co-worker will do one."

"Why ya seperatin' us? Me and Ali can just tell ya together." Sarah didn't want to leave Ali's side.

"No." Sparks was firm.

The little room was all gray. There was one folding table and three chairs. Sarah sat down nearest the back wall. She noticed a mirrored glass to her right.

"Is somebody gonna be standin' there watchin'?"

"No ma'am. We are tapin' it." The man pointed over his left shoulder to a tiny camera in the corner of the ceiling.

"Oh."

The man was Reginald Dorsey. He was a dark man of African American descent. His glasses were horn-rimmed black. He was wearing a baby blue collared shirt; something you could find at Wal-Mart, along with khakis. "So Ms...Buckman...tell me what happened last night."

"Well we were just sittin' there talkin' and then she got up from the table..."

"You mean Ms. Carter?"

"Yeah, me and Ali were talkin'. She got up and went to the pool room and then Monya Tarville came runnin' at me and told me that he took her. I jumped up, ran out the door, got in my car, and followed 'em. Once he stopped on the side of the road I rode up on 'em real slow..."

"How did you know it was Ms. Carter in there?"

"Oh, uh, Erica Smalley told me and then I told her to call Sparks right quick, but I called him too. He was on the phone with her when I got through to him. I stayed on

Renee Black

the phone with him until they stopped. I let him know where to send the officers. Anyhow, so I got up behind 'em and parked. The cops showed up and so I knew he would be pre-occupied with them. So what I did was, I snuck up to the back of the truck and climbed in. The cops were sayin' nobody move, and I thought they might be talkin' about me but I had to get to Ali. I just wanted to talk him down, ya know, 'cause there's no reason for anybody to get hurt."

"But…all of this is because he knocked over your bank a while back, right?" Dorsey began writing in his notebook.

"Yeah, he robbed it. He took us hostage. He raped her, and now she's pregnant with his baby. See? That's why I had to make sure she didn't get hurt."

"So when he took ya'll hostage he didn't rape you?"

"No sir. He's her ex-boyfriend see, and…well he got mad because she said she wasn't into him anymore."

"He raped her because she rejected him?"

"Well…yes and no."

Dorsey slid his glasses down to the bridge of his nose. He peered at her over top of them. "Please continue."

"Look, me and Ali are a couple, ok. He got mad because she said I was better in bed than he was, so I guess he wanted to prove her wrong but he did just the opposite."

"Ms. Buckman why would she have egged him on?"

Reluctantly, Sarah told the truth. "No…she didn't. When he took off the mask and she saw him she knew who he was. He told her she was lookin' good and all this stuff. She kinda ignored him and then he noticed how she was lookin' at me. He got mad about it and told her that dick is what she wanted. She said I was the best she ever had and it infuriated him. She told the truth so she wouldn't hurt my feelin's, but she ended up hurtin' herself in the long run 'cause he raped her for it."

"And now she's pregnant with his child?"

"Yes sir. That's what I told him, and promised he could be part of the baby's life, but he had to be alive and let Ali go."

"He said he'd already let her go when you climbed up in the truck."

"Yes, he had, but I didn't know that."

"You must really love her to go up against a man with a gun."

"Well…" Sarah looked down at the floor. "I do sir, with all my heart."

"Alright, just sit here. I'll be back." He got up and exited the room. He left Sarah to think about the events and how lucky they both were to make it out alive.

Ali was nervous. When Sparks walked in she was chewing on her nail beds.

"Ms. Carter…we have arrested Ms. Buckman for raping you."

"What? No! You can't do that! Now what am I gonna do?"

Recommended Readings

Titles by Karen D. Neal

Grey Family Preys
Grey Family Preys 2: The Flip Side
She Me We
He Him They

Titles by LJ Thomas

The Journey: Domestic Violence
Bad Nerves: All About MS and Stuff
And I Trusted You
What Is This World Coming To?
AMB Shorts

Titles by Aija M. Butler

Hood Bound
Under Lock and Key
Mirrors of Deception
Rebirth of My Soul
Scorned

Future Titles to look for

Kidnapped In Love by LJ Thomas and Karen D. Neal
Grey Family Preys 3: New Beginnings by Karen D. Neal
Hidden Desires 2: Finally Lived by Renee Black